The Pit List Murder

Renee George

The Pit List Murder

(Barkside of the Moon Mysteries Book 3)

ISBN-13: 978-1-947177-16-1

Pit Bulls are Sweet . . .and that's no mystery!

Lily Mason and her adorable pittie Smooshie both have a nose for murder, but this is one cougar-Shifter who would give her left paw to never find another dead body. All she wants is to enjoy a simple life in her new town, her fixer-upper house, while working a job she loves. Besides, the mystery of whether Parker Knowles, her boss at the rescue shelter, will or won't finally ask her out gives Lily plenty to keep her guessing.

But when an abandoned pit bull puppy leads Lily and Smooshie to the corpse of a local Lothario, she is once again drawn into the seedier side of small town living. Even though she's warned off the case by the local sheriff, Lily is determined to find the killer. It doesn't help matters that more nasty notes are showing up around town, making Lily wonder if the two things are connected.

Lily and Smooshie need to crack the case of the dead Don Juan, while navigating what it means to live in an all human town, before the secrets of the people she cares for are exposed.

DEDICATION

For all the furbabies who have been

rescued or need rescuing.

May you all find your forever home.

Adopt Don't Shop

.

CONTENTS

Chapter One 7
Chapter Two 25
Chapter Three 35
Chapter Four 47
Chapter Five 59
Chapter Six 69
Chapter Seven 85
Chapter Eight 93
Chapter Nine 105
Chapter Ten 118
Chapter Eleven 130
Chapter Twelve 141
Chapter Thirteen 154
Chapter Fourteen 162
Chapter Fifteen 172
Chapter Sixteen 183
Chapter Seventeen 194
Chapter Eighteen 208
Chapter Nineteen 220
Chapter Twenty 233
Chapter Twenty-one 244
Chapter Twenty-two 262

ACKNOWLEDGMENTS

I am proudly a Bully Hero for Missouri Pit Bull Rescue. It takes a lot to keep a shelter running, and this organization goes above and beyond when it comes to taking care of these rescued babies. I encourage everyone who loves dogs to donate to this group (www.mopitbullrescue.org) as they build their new shelter that will allow them to house even more rescues until they can be placed in foster or forever homes.

Second, I have to thank two hardcore ladies who were with me every step of this book, Michele Bardsley and Robbin Clubb. I don't know what I'd do without either you.

Third, I want to thank my niece Jeanna Settles, who really pays attention and calls me out if I screw up a timeline or forget how many kids a character has. I love you, darling!

Fourth, I need to kiss the ass of my editor Kelli Collins who turned the edits around on this book in record breaking time. You are a complete rock star!

Fifth, I want to give a shout out to my rebel readers. I'm so much better with you than without you! Thank you for being such great fans and readers.

CHAPTER ONE

MY MOTHER USED to say, "I'd rather be disappointed than have no hope." For the longest time, I didn't understand what she'd meant by those words. After she and my father were killed, hope was a scarce commodity. I'd come to expect that bad things happened, that I would never be able to command my own life. Growing up in a town full of Shifters and witches, I learned early on that my worth was based on my contribution to the community. I had nothing to offer the town. At least nothing they valued. I am small for a werecougar and economically challenged. Neither one of those things will win you most popular in a Shifter town.

After I quit high school to support my little brother, I'd worked as a waitress, a dishwasher, and a cashier. My last job before I put my hometown in the rearview mirror had been a stocker at the local grocer. In other words, all minimum-wage jobs that required no skills other than good shoes and a strong back. The only thing I owned was my beat up mini-truck Martha. I think that's why I cherish her so much.

Anyhow, like I said before, I hadn't known what Mom meant about a lack of hope and its correlation to disappointment...until I moved to Moonrise, Missouri. Now, I was full of hope and, unfortunately, I felt the keen sting of disappointment all too sharply as a result.

Two months had passed since I'd revealed my Shifter secret to Parker Knowles—my boss at Moonrise's pit bull shelter. I know, ironic, right? A cat that helps dogs, ha.

After I'd shown Parker my true nature, he'd kissed me in the woods near a great oak I'd dubbed "the money tree." Why? Because that's where I found stolen bank money and had gotten a $120,000 finder's fee. I donated half to the rescue, and Parker hadn't wasted time in getting the foundation poured on the new kennels. The walls were up, and it had a roof. I sometimes wished I would have donated all the money, but the other half of the money paid off the mortgage on my property, which meant I didn't have to get a second job away from the pit bull rescue shelter.

You'd think that breath-stealing kiss meant that Parker was down with the whole paranormal thing, but you'd be wrong. At least he hadn't told me to stop coming to work. The rescue shelter and my companion, a large and loving pit bull named Smooshie, were the only two things that kept me putting one foot in front of the other these days.

I didn't know what to do about the distance growing between Parker and me. He'd confessed he was falling in love with me, kissed me, and then he'd walked away. I supposed finding out the girl you wanted to be with was a giant cat some of the time could mess up anyone.

The way Parker avoided me most of the time, I wondered if maybe I should take Ryan Petry, the local veterinarian, up on his offer to work at his office. I loved working at the shelter, but I was beginning to believe my presence there was too much additional stress for Parker. He already suffered from PTSD from his military service, and twice since he's known me, he'd had a gun pulled on him. Finding out that I'm not exactly human and no stranger to violence could not have had a positive influence on his feelings for me.

"Should I wear the studs or the hoops?" Reggie asked.

Reggie's question drew me out of my thoughts and back to the present moment. I was with my two human besties, Reggie Crawford, a local doc and the town coroner, and Nadine Booth, a deputy sheriff and my uncle's main squeeze.

Reggie's black shoulder-length hair was pressed straight. She wore a blue and turquoise wrap blouse and a pair of black jeans with blue suede pumps. She held a small diamond up to one ear and a gold quarter-inch-wide hoop earring near the other.

"That shirt is crying for those hoops," Nadine Booth said before I could say "wear the studs."

Both women were flashier than me, so it should have come as no surprise that the big gold hoops got both their votes. Reggie was a general surgeon, and she'd taken on the role of coroner after the last one, Tom Jones, had been arrested for murder. And attempted murder—mine.

I stifled a shiver as goose bumps raised on my arms. I hated even thinking about Tom, but since his trial was going to start in six weeks, he'd been on my mind a lot. I'd been grilled upside down and sideways by the prosecuting attorney in preparation for my testimony. I still can't believe Tom had recanted his confession. It made me sick to think about how he'd nearly killed me.

Nadine put her hand on my shoulder. "Earth to Lily. Where'd you go there, sweetie?" She brushed her luminous brown hair off her shoulder, the LED lighting from Reggie's mirror making her pale-green eyes glow. At that moment, she reminded me of a Shifter.

I shook off the sudden melancholy and forced a smile. "Nowhere." Both women gave me a skeptical look. "I'm fine. Really."

Reggie's daughter, CeCe, was graduating from Moonrise High School in a few weeks. Nadine and I both agreed to go with her since it would be the first time she'd have to see her ex-jerkface since the divorce one year earlier. I had planned on attending anyways because Addison "Addy" Newton, a teenager who volunteered at the shelter, was also graduating. Addy had a shaky past, but over the past several months, he'd proven himself to be a really great kid. The fact that he reminded me of my younger brother Danny only added to my fondness.

"How do I look?" Reggie asked.

"You look beautiful," I said. "And you're going to be drop-dead gorgeous at the graduation, and that ex of yours will have no choice but to eat his heart out."

Reggie snorted. "That would require him to have a heart." The middle-aged doctor was only seven years older than me, which put her in her early-forties. My nonhuman status made me look a lot younger. Still, Reggie's fine lines gave her a grace I wish I had. I blinked when I realized her grace wasn't the only thing I envied. I also wished I was human. It would certainly make my life less complicated.

Reggie smoothed down her already smooth hair. "I'm nervous about seeing David." She leaned toward her mirror and wiped the bottom right corner of her lip in a move to fix her burgundy lipstick that didn't need fixing. "I moved all the way across the state to get away from him."

"If he looks at you cross-eyed, I'll throat punch him." I gave her a feral smile.

Nadine nodded. "And if he gives you any trouble, I'll show him how effective a Taser is in controlling unruly ex-husbands."

Reggie laughed. "I'm simultaneously grateful and afraid that you two are my friends."

Nadine bumped her shoulder against Reggie's. "We love you, too."

Both Reggie and Nadine helped to make life bearable. Especially since Parker had built the wall of silence between us. He and I had been close before he found out about my dual nature, so the lack of contact was deeply painful. We kept our conversations short, sweet, and mostly business related. I missed having coffee and toast with him in the mornings. I missed the occasional spaghetti dinner he would make for me. But most of all, I just missed *him*. Sure, I saw him almost every day, but his emotional withdrawal made me ache.

"Who are you thinking about?" Nadine asked.

"What makes you think I'm thinking about someone?"

"You have a wistful look." The young deputy narrowed her eyes at me. "Almost pining."

"I don't pine," I said, irritated at how easy I was to read.

"You really have the look down pat for someone who doesn't pine," Reggie said.

I stood up. "You two got your signals crossed is all." I grabbed my purse. "Are we going to Dally's Tavern or are we staying here like a bunch of clucking hens ready to lay eggs?"

Nadine laughed. "People are going to start mistaking you for a local if you keep talking like that. I can't wait to tell Buzz what you said."

I gave her a wry look. "Who do you think taught me the line?"

Reggie grabbed her purse. "Well, I for one have no intention of laying eggs. Let's get out of here before we start molting."

****

Dally's Tavern & Grill on State Street was packed wall to wall with men and women of all ages. Since Nix's Bar burned down, it had become more than a college hang-out. The students had no choice but to share their space with all of the locals—in other words, the not-so-young-and-perky crowd.

Tuesday was ladies' night, which meant cheap drinks and food, and it was a standing girls' night for Reggie, Nadine, and me.

"Buzz texted," Nadine said after we grabbed a table. She held up the phone and showed me a picture of my female pit bull, Smooshie, holding a squeaky monkey in her mouth.

I resisted the urge to pet the picture. "I think Smooshie has a crush on Buzz."

"Her and every other woman in town," Nadine said. She smiled, but I could see the real concern in her expression.

"Oh, Nadine," Reggie chided. "That man's crazy about you, and you know it."

She shrugged. "I don't know why I said that." Her eyes darkened as she lowered her gaze to the table. She rapped her knuckles on the wood top. "I think we need a round of drinks."

"Heck yeah," Reggie said. "Now you're talking." She waved her hand at a wandering waiter, a young guy named Donnie.

"Hey, ladies. What can I get you all to drink tonight?" Donnie stood over six feet tall, and he was built like a swimmer, large upper body, narrow waist and hips. He had the kind of smile that could and probably did break hearts.

Reggie leaned forward, appreciating the view. "I'll take a Gin Rickey." She glanced at me.

"Beer," I said.

"I'll take a peach wine cooler," Nadine said.

I snorted.

"What? They're delicious," she said. Her raised right brow dared me to say different.

I wasn't taking the bait. "I'd love some triple-cheese, chicken-bacon nachos," I told Donnie.

He nodded, flashing his flirty smile at the three of us.

Reggie leaned forward and murmured, "That boy is dangerous." She finished the statement off with a grin. "They didn't make 'em like him when I was young."

Nadine shook her head at Reggie. "You need a date and soon."

Our friend ran her finger along the edge of her hoop earring. "I'm too old to start over again." She looked at me. "Don't you think?"

"You're never too old to live your life to the fullest." I wished I could take my own advice.

"Besides," Nadine added. "You're gorgeous." She shook her head. "This ex of yours has really done your head in if you think otherwise." Donnie passed by at that moment, hands free of his drink tray. Nadine stopped him. "Hey, you think my friend Reggie here is beautiful, right?"

"Nadine!" Reggie admonished. She looked at Donnie. "I'm sorry," she told him. "My friend is trying to make me feel better."

The corner of Donnie's mouth curled into a smile. "For the record, you *are* beautiful, and I'm all for making beautiful women feel better." Someone called his name a few tables down from us. He smiled and nodded. "Duty calls." He winked at Reggie. "But you just holler if you need anything. Anything at all."

After he left, Reggie let out the breath she'd been holding. Nadine and I both waited as she composed herself. I really thought Reg was going to give Nadine what for, but instead, she started giggling, which made me giggle, and then Nadine joined in.

Reggie fanned herself. "That kid is something else. I might need to find a block of ice to sit on."

"You know he's twenty-four," Nadine said. "He's getting his master's degree at Southeast Missouri State University, and he teaches as an adjunct at the community college here in town."

I looked at Nadine. "And how do you know all this?"

Nadine laughed. "He called about a break-in at his house a few days ago. I took the call. He's a chatty charmer."

"Did you catch the thief?"

"Turned out nothing was taken," Nadine said. "You know...he just lives a mile or two down the road from you on the Jessup property. He's renting to own." She wiggled her brows. "Maybe that boy could break your cold streak." She shrugged. "Unless you're still holding out for Parker."

Before I had to defend my choice not to date anyone, we were interrupted.

"Ladies," a male voice crooned from a few feet away.

I looked up and groaned. Jock Simmons was one of the few people in town I really disliked. And a drunk Jock was ten times worse than a sober one. Jock was a local lawyer. He was married to the only other paid employee at the rescue shelter, Theresa Simmons. Theresa was also the sheriff's daughter, which always made me wonder why Jock would push the envelope the way he did. The man had a reputation for tomcatting, and I suspected he sometimes took a hand to his wife. I'd seen bruises on Theresa more than once.

As if he read my mind, he put his arm around Reggie's shoulders. He was angled over us enough to encroach on our personal space even more. His breath reeked of bourbon. "You three are looking purtier than five-dollar bills on quarter night."

Reggie's dark eyes widened at me.

He ogled Nadine, his eyes glassy as he looked purposefully at her breasts. "You should come dance with me, darling."

Nadine rolled her eyes. "You should walk away, Jock."

I stood up and bared my teeth. "Bye, Jock," I said with a hint of menace.

He raised his hands in the air, and Reggie leaned away from him, her body tense and ready to react if he tried to put his arm around her again.

"I'm just trying to be neighborly," Jock said. He glared at me then walked away.

Nadine leaned over. "He makes me wish I'd brought my gun."

Reggie and I both laughed. Donnie came back with our drinks. He gave me another smile. "Your nachos will be out shortly."

"Thanks." I took a sip of beer.

To Reggie, he said, "Is there anything else I can get for you?"

She blushed and shook her head. "I'm good."

"I'd sure like to find out." And with that, he walked away.

Reggie smiled as she drank her Gin Ricky. I was all for her enjoying a flirtatious comment from a good-looking guy. So, I tried not to stare as the woman with shoulder-length, straight brown hair strolled up behind the waiter. She seemed familiar, but I hadn't met her before. I had a memory for faces. Most likely, I'd seen her at the store or something.

Donnie's face registered surprise as she slid her arms around him and tried to shove her fingers down the front of his jeans.

He dropped the empty tray he held and rounded on her. "Rachel," he said, his tone gentle and placating. "I'm working right now." He was quiet enough that I shouldn't have been able to hear the conversation, especially over the rest of the noise in the bar, but when you grow up with supernatural hearing, you learn quickly how to tune out and tune in different sounds. Right now, I was curiously distracted by the waiter and his unwanted guest.

Rachel—wearing jeans, cowgirl boots, and a western shirt—giggled and tried to grab him again. "Come on, Donnie. I miss you. Don't you miss me?"

He looked around as he picked up the tray and worked hard to keep a few feet between him and this Rachel. "What are you doing here?"

Rachel's smile faded. "You said you'd call me." Her hand went up as if to reach out to him, but Donnie stepped back. "You can't do this to me," she hissed. "I won't be ignored."

Lacy Evans interrupted the hushed conversation by stumbling, drunk, between them. "Donnie Doyle!" she squealed. "Where have you been all night, handsome?" She squished his face between her palms. "Damn, your face makes me want to kiss your momma."

He gently disengaged himself from Lacy, and I noted that Rachel had disappeared. Well, that was the end of that eavesdrop. I could care less about what Lacy had to say. She was Freda Downing's daughter. Freda was my uncle Buzz's waitress, and she worked nearly every shift at The Cat's Meow. She treated me with a kind of wariness, not that I could blame her. As a result of a witch in my family tree, it was hard for people to keep secrets from me, and Freda had a lot of secrets, especially when it came to her daughter. I try not to judge people. However, Lacy was a single mom who took her partying more seriously than she took her responsibility as a parent. It made it hard not to judge.

"Ugh, I can't stand her," Nadine said, echoing my thoughts.

I shook my head. "She makes it hard to like her."

"Try impossible." Nadine cast a distrustful gaze at Lacy. "There is something truly wrong with that girl."

Donnie was engaged in conversation with another woman now, a short, curvy brunette. It was almost as intense as the one he'd had with Rachel, but they were farther away, and there were too many conversations going on between them and me.

"Who is that?"

"Do you think I know everyone in town?" Nadine asked.

I sort of did. I hid my grin. "You could have just said you don't know."

"I don't know." She laughed. "We have almost twenty thousand people living here. Did you know everyone back in your hometown?"

"No," I said. I'd made the mistake that a lot of people make when they assume everyone in a small town knows everyone. It just felt like more often than not it was true.

Reggie slapped her palms down on the table. "We have other, more important matters to discuss tonight, ladies. Like how I'm going to face my ex-jerk."

Reggie was right. Thinking about Lacy Evans was a huge waste of a girls' night out. "When is the dirtbag driving down?" I asked.

"The day before graduation. He rented a room at the Moonrise Inn. He wants CeCe to have dinner with him that night." She wrung her hands together. "I haven't seen that man in over a year. Not since we signed the divorce papers."

I put my hand over hers. "You never needed him, Reg. And he sure as hell didn't deserve you. You are strong, beautiful, independent, and successful. You've made a life for yourself and your daughter, and you did it without him."

"Damn straight," Nadine added. "You are one tough chick. And if that man even bats an eyelash wrong, I've got shovels, and Lils can bring the black trash bags." She winked. "And since I'm a cop, I'll make sure his disappearance goes unsolved."

Reggie laughed. "All right," she said. "How can I worry with friends like you?"

"You can't," Nadine said brightly. "It's impossible."

A woman slurred out the words, "Get the hell away from me." I looked up to see Lacy and Jock near the pool tables. Lacy had her hand up as if to slap him, and Jock's fingers were wrapped around her wrist.

"What's wrong?" Jock asked, his voice dripping with condescension. "Am I not married enough for you?" He laughed when Lacy's eyes widened. His tone was hushed as he leaned in close to her and added, "Who do I have to kill to get you in bed?"

Lacy was Jock's secretary. He was in a position of power over her, and I couldn't watch as he tried to bully her into doing something she didn't want to do.

I jumped up from my chair and made a beeline for the duo, surprising myself and them with my righteous anger. Lacy had been having an affair with Tom Jones, the man who'd tried to kill me. He was also the father of the son she often ignored. And while the young woman had made some questionable life choices, Jock had no right to throw it in her face or use her past as a way to coerce her into having sex with him. I focused my fury on him as I approached. "You get your hands off her right now, or I swear I'll break every one of your fingers."

Jock looked sideways and down at me as if to gauge my threat level. Something in my eyes must have registered as high threat because he let go of her wrist. He threw his hands up in mock surrender. "We're just having a friendly conversation here."

Lacy looked more rattled than I'd ever seen her. I put intention in my words, calling upon my grandmother's curse, a type of honesty magic, weak but effective if the person I was talking to wanted the truth revealed. "Are you two having a friendly conversation?"

She shook her head. "No, we're not. I want Jock to leave me alone." She blinked as if she couldn't believe the words that came out of her mouth. I think she was more shocked than her boss.

"I'm just trying to buy a lady a drink," Jock said, irritation plain in his tone. Without any argument, though, he turned on his heel and walked away.

"Everything okay over here?" Donnie asked.

Lacy's dark expression brightened. "Nothing a little of you couldn't fix."

I hoped my eyes didn't roll, but sometimes it's automatic, especially when the situation warrants it. "I'll see you around," I said.

I glanced over at my table, Reggie and Nadine both stared at me with what-the-heck expressions. I felt Lacy's hand, cool and slightly clammy, touch my arm. I looked back at her. A tight smile greeted me. "Thanks, Lily," she said. "I mean it."

I walked back to the table, a little numb at Lacy's genuine gratitude for my intervention.

"Is Lacy up to no good?" Nadine asked when I sat down.

I took a sip of my beer. "She's a lot." I wiped at the sweat on the bottle. "But no one should have to put up with Jock."

Nadine and Regina nodded. Nadine said, "If being a dick was illegal, they would lock Jock up and throw away the key."

Reggie raised a brow. "I'm not sure Lacy is much better."

I stared across the room as she slid into a booth with a couple of young frat boys. "Regardless, she still doesn't deserve to be harassed."

Nadine and Reggie held up their glasses. "True story," Nadine said.

I clinked my beer with their drinks. "Yep."

CHAPTER TWO

THE NEXT WEEK, WE'D SKIPPED girls' night because Nadine got called into work and Reggie had some senior thing at CeCe's school. Besides, it gave me extra study time for my GED exam on Saturday. When the end of the week rolled around, my stomach and brains were in knots. But, I liked Fridays at the shelter because they were always busy. It felt good to throw myself into work, especially these days. Performing multiple tasks kept my mind occupied with things other than Parker and my stupid test. Today, I was inputting donations and purchases, and keeping my fingers crossed that the donations would keep us in the green and out of the red. Even with the bank reward I'd shared with Parker to build on the new site, money was still tight for the shelter.

Math had never been a strength, but with a calculator, I managed to make the numbers add up. Most of the time. I narrowed my gaze on the total column of the table I'd been filling in. The amount of money in the petty cash didn't match. It was off by negative ten dollars.

The loud chorus of barking alerted me that Keith Porter had returned with Star, a beautiful gray pittie we'd taken in a couple months earlier. She'd been overbred and half-starved when she'd arrived. Now, she was a healthy forty-four pounds, a much smaller dog than my Smooshie. I leaned back in my chair and looked out the office door. "Hey, Keith. Can I see you a moment?"

Keith, a lanky fellow with a poorly developed beard, shaggy brown hair, but unusual green-blue eyes that made him almost handsome, ducked his head inside the office.

"What's up, Lils?"

I gestured past him with a nod. "How's the girl?"

"She's still skittish, but she's getting healthier all the time."

I smiled. "I'm glad." Star's shy personality and her inability to get along with other dogs made her hard to place. We'd even had to put her kennel in a room by itself. I felt a kinship with her in a way. It's a hard way to live being scared all the time.

"Did you need something?" Keith asked. I'd worked the day shift with Keith and with Jerry Atwell, a volunteer whose full-time job was firefighting. His wife had been in the hospital with pneumonia the week before, but she was home now, and Jerry had resumed his shifts at the shelter.

I'd noticed Keith had started volunteering to work at times when Theresa Simmons didn't work. Theresa had confided in me that she and Keith had been having an affair for some time. This new distancing told me it might be over. Keith was younger than Theresa by a decade. I wasn't throwing stones. I was older than Parker by as many years and more. But I'd always worried that Keith would end up on the losing end of the relationship. Theresa, no matter how poorly Jock treated her, had no intentions of leaving him.

"Did you get some money out of petty cash for something and not log it?"

"Shoot. Yes. I took a ten out this morning to get coffee and disposable cups." He indicated the new canister and stack of cups on a small table in the corner of the office. "Sorry about that."

"No worries. It's ten bucks. I just like to have everything add up. Do you have the receipt?"

Keith shoved his hands into his pockets, pulling out keys, change, a phone. Everything but a receipt. "I'm sorry, Lily. It might be out in my car."

I shook my head. "I'll write it in, Keith. Don't worry about it. Just keep the receipt next time and log the expense."

He smiled. "You got it."

Smooshie, who'd been asleep at my feet, must have sensed my mood. She shoved her large head under my hand, her wet nose brushing my palm, and whined. I looked from the computer, where I'd been inputting costs of supplies, to my enthusiastic baby. Her coloring was what was called red and white, though the red was more a rusty brown. Her face was white, with red framing her expressive brown eyes.

"Hey, big girl." Her butt wiggled with excitement while her tail whacked the side of the desk with a loud *thwack, thwack, thwack*. She was definitely feeling neglected. "I'm sorry." I scratched her behind the ear, leaned over and wrapped my arms around her waist while she shoved her head between my knees and under the chair. Her tail brushed my hair, and I smiled.

When I sat up, Keith was grinning, but he wasn't looking at me. I followed the direction of his gaze to find Parker Knowles standing in the office doorway staring at me with a strange expression I couldn't decipher.

I swallowed the hard knot in my throat. "Hi."

He nodded to me. "Hi." His dog Elvis stood behind him, ready to be there for Parker if he became stressed. Elvis was a trained service animal, a pit bull-Great Dane mix, which made him almost four feet tall, and the beautiful blue-furred beast probably outweighed me by a good ten pounds.

Smooshie's ears perked up as she quickly propelled her stocky body past Parker and promptly shoved her nose right up under Elvis' tail. The taller dog stood perfectly still, waiting for someone to make her stop.

"Smoosh," I said sharply. She looked around Parker's hip at me. "Manners," I told her. "We don't stick our noses uninvited into butts that don't belong to us."

Keith laughed. Parker said, "I didn't realize you both like to stick your noses in butts..."

"Don't be cute," I said. But, gosh, too late. Parker was a little under six feet, built like a heavyweight boxer, and he had the bluest eyes I'd ever seen. The kind of eyes a woman could get lost in.

"I'm off, boss," Keith said to Parker as he eased past him. "Jerry's my ride, and he has a shift at the firehouse tonight." Keith threw me a boyish grin. "See you later, Lils."

I waved. "See ya."

Parker had moved all the way into the room now, but Elvis stayed out in the hall. I imagined he'd had his fill of Smooshie's brand of hello. Parker leaned against the wall, his arms crossed over his chest. "How's everything?"

I assumed he was talking about the center's finances. "We are staying afloat." I rotated my chair to face him. "How's the build going?" He'd been hands-on with the construction at the new property.

"Good." He shook his head. "Good. Wish it was progressing a little faster, but it's getting there. You should go with me sometime and check it out."

I nodded. "Sure." My pulse sped up. This might have been the longest conversation we'd shared since my revelation. He'd confessed his feelings for me, but in the same breath, he told me he needed time to "process" everything. In other words, seeing me transform into a cougar and rip a man's throat out had freaked him out.

I guess I couldn't blame him, but in a way I did. I'd spent my entire life as an outsider in my own community. With Moonrise, I'd finally found a place where I belonged. Or at least, it felt that way most of the time. Maybe it was time for us to talk. Really talk.

"Hey, we should get some—"

"What's that?" Parker took two quick steps toward me. Fast enough that I had to brace myself to keep from moving into a defensive posture. He picked up a pamphlet near the computer. "Are you planning on going to college?"

The pamphlet was for the veterinarian assistant program at Two Hills Community College. "Ryan dropped that off for me," was the wrong thing to say. The lobes of Parker's ears turned red, and his nostrils flared with anger.

"Ryan, huh?" He kept his voice low and calm. I saw his struggle to keep his breathing slow and even. He wasn't fooling Elvis, who moved in quick, nudging his big head between Parker's hand and hip. He wasn't fooling me, either.

I sighed. "I'm thinking about taking some classes in the fall." First, I had to get my GED, but Parker didn't know I hadn't finished high school. I hadn't told anyone in Moonrise, except Nadine—not out of shame, but because I didn't want to explain why. I only told Nadine because the test was seven hours long, and she agreed to dogsit for me when I took it. I'd quit school to become my brother's guardian my senior year. My parents getting murdered had put an end to my dreams of graduating and going off to college to become a medical doctor. Still, I'd been reluctant to share my lack of education with Parker.

"That's great." He forced a smile. Our gazes locked, and my stomach dipped. The tension around his eyes eased. "Really. I think it's great."

"Nothing's set in stone." I shrugged. Why didn't I just tell him that I'd signed up for the GED course?

"You're too smart not to go," Parker said.

I took the compliment. "Thanks." I know I'm smart. I've devoured every medical book and journal I could get my hands on over the past seventeen years. It was my only consolation in a life I'd never meant to lead.

Parker's scent, that of mint and honey, blossomed in the room. For a moment, I closed my eyes, let go of my control, and inhaled deeply.

When I opened my eyes, objects were crisper and colors more vivid.

Parker, his brows raised, took a step back.

I turned away from him, blinking as I pulled my inner cat back from the brink. "I'm sorry."

"Lily—"

The phone rang before he could say more. Parker, his expression relieved, grabbed the phone. "Moonrise Pit Bull Rescue," he said. "How can I help you?"

Saved by the bell, or ringer, in this case. When I wasn't in cougar form, I wasn't nearly as attuned to the world around me, but I could still hear better than humans. I listened for the voice on the other end of the line.

"Hello," a woman said. Her voice was shaky and raspy. She was elderly. "Is this the dog place? The one for those pit bulls?"

"Yes, ma'am," Parker replied patiently. "This is the Moonrise Pit Bull Rescue Center."

"Is that you, Parker?"

I recognized the voice now. "It's Opal Dixon," I said quietly to Parker.

Opal and her sister Pearl were frequent flyers at my uncle Buzz's diner, The Cat's Meow. They ate breakfast there every day. Opal, whose hair was white and fluffy like a cotton ball, was a no-nonsense lady. She also had a sharp tongue, which she frequently used on her sister.

Parker nodded. "How can I help you, ma'am?"

"I've got a dog here at my place. Still a puppy, I think. He's the same color as Lily Mason's dog only smaller, which is why I called you all. Poor thing's filthy. Has some kind of dried schmutz on his fur, and he's about half-starved. I could play chopsticks on his ribs. He is sweet as a peach though. He hasn't stopped licking Pearl since she brought him inside. Is he yours?"

"He is now." Parker's brows narrowed, and his blue eyes darkened. "I'll be right out, Ms. Dixon. Can I get your address?"

"How do you know my name? I didn't say who I was." Her tone was cautious and suspicious, and a little bit scared.

Parker winced. "You said the dog was with your sister Pearl, so I assumed."

"Oh."

I grinned and shook my head. Opal gave Parker her address. After he said goodbye, he gave me a look. "Do you want to come with me?"

His invitation gave me another surge of hope. "Sure. You think your dad would keep an eye on Smoosh?"

Parker smiled. "I bet he won't say no. He has a soft spot for the two of you."

CHAPTER THREE

I SPENT THE RIDE staring out the passenger window of Parker's large dually pickup truck. The Dixon sisters lived out on a rural gravel road, and Parker had been unsurprisingly silent. I metaphorically kicked myself for once again revealing the animal inside me that lurked beneath the surface. I'd freaked him out.

But then again, why had he invited me along for the ride? Was he trying to make an effort to reconnect? "I'd have guessed Opal and Pearl for town dwellers," I said. Small talk was a safe place to start.

Parker shrugged. "I've never been to their place, but my dad says it's something to behold. I thought you might want to see it as well."

"Tell me." A little smile formed on my lips. "Do they have a mansion or something?" I leaned forward, my hand touching the bumpy dashboard, warmed by the sun. "They're rich, aren't they? I'd have never guessed. Are they like that one mother and daughter?" I snapped my fingers. "Gray Gardens, or something like that."

Parker chuckled. It made me stupidly happy. "You have a wild imagination, Lily Mason, but I don't even think *you* will be able to guess what we'll find when we reach the sisters' lair."

I rubbed my hands together. The plot thickened. "Oooo. A lair." I looked over at him. "I'm sad about the abandoned dog, but I have to say, I'm glad I get to go on this adventure with you."

His lips pursed then relaxed. "Me too."

We turned down a long gravel drive, and while my mind had scrolled through the many things I'd find, I was ill-prepared for what I actually saw.

"Wow."

Plastic palm trees lined the last fifty feet of the narrow drive that led to a white fifty-foot double-wide trailer.

We parked and got out of the truck.

The front yard on either side had a white picket fence border, and inside there were two lawn chairs and probably three dozen pink flamingo lawn ornaments. Strings of colorful lights played over the top of the fenced yard in a canopy of green wires with hanging yellow, red, green, and blue bulbs. There was a signpost arm pointing south that said, "Miami, 1,095 miles." There was another sign on the wall of the white trailer that said, "Age is just a number, but the aches and pains are real."

Opal Dixon, an elderly woman about my height—which means short, right around five feet tall—opened the door. Her snowball-white hair was messy like a bird's nest.

"Welcome to Casa de Dixon. Don't just stand their gawking." She jerked her thumb over her shoulder. "Pup's in the house."

I wouldn't call the tin cup I lived in a house, but the word applied here even if it was just a trailer.

Parker nodded, and we followed her inside.

The spaciousness surprised me. I figured the two ladies would have accumulated a lot of junk over the years, and that the place would be wall to wall with knickknacks and antique furniture. I was wrong. The Miami retirement theme was carried inside. A few tropical plants, wicker furniture, sandy-colored walls with accents of pale blues and greens, a bamboo desk with a bill box, stationary, and an assortment of pens, and the living room had a woven-palm ceiling fan. Even though it was seventy-two degrees outside, the heater ran, and it made the place feel even more tropical.

Aside from the Miami theme, I noticed a lack of pictures on the walls. No awkward family photos. No children or grandchildren. I knew from Buzz that Opal had never married, but Pearl had been widowed twenty years ago. They had each other.

That was it. But to have one person in your life that you can count on wholly and completely, who had your back through thick and thin, I knew that was enough. Or at least, I thought it would be. I'd never had anyone in my life like that. Not even my best friend from back home, Haze Kinsey. I knew if I called, she'd come running, but I wanted someone in my life who would come even if I was too proud to call. Someone who would just know.

Opal must have caught me examining her digs, because she said, "Pearl wanted to retire in Florida. This was our compromise." She led us down the hall. "Dog's in the spare room."

I detected the slight metal scent of blood. "Is the dog injured?"

Opal gave me a strange look. "I don't think so. It's a bit dirty from clomping about in the mud and weeds, maybe scratched up some, but mostly it's just hungry. Well, it was. I gave it some leftovers from the fridge."

Parker put his hand on my arm and said quietly, "What is it?"

I shook my head. Opal opened the door. In the corner of the room, half under a pile of cushy throw blankets, a puppy peeked his head up to stare at the two strangers who had disturbed his sleep. He had a red patch of fur over his left eye, the opposite of Smoosh. His cheekbones were prominent, and I could readily see his shoulder blades and ribs. There was a distinct lack of muscle tone from malnourishment.

I clenched my fists to hold down my anger. Slowly, I crouched in front of the poor baby. He whimpered, dropping his head on the blanket. Dogs had a strange reaction to me. They tended to be calmer when I was around. I think it had to do with me being a Shifter, but since I'd never been around domesticated animals that didn't speak English before Moonrise, I had no way of knowing for sure.

The puppy crawled on his belly toward me until his nose touched my fingers. "There, there, little guy," I said. I gently picked him up, cradling his body in my arms. He probably weighed between fifteen and twenty pounds, not nearly enough to fill out his tall frame. His fur was crusted with mud and debris, so I manually checked him, running my fingers down every inch of his fur, knocking off clumps of the dried dirt, until I was satisfied he wasn't hurt.

"Is he injured?" Parker asked.

The blood scent was still present, but it wasn't fresh. "Not that I can see." I turned his collar to look at his tab. "He's had vaccinations. One of Ryan's patients. He can tell us who the owner is."

Parker's bright blue eyes were livid. "There's no excuse for neglect."

"I agree." I stroked the pup's back to soothe his nerves.

"I fed it and gave it some water," Opal said. "But Pearl and I can't take care of a dog. The place is too small for us to have a critter under our feet. The last thing I need is a broken hip or worse."

"Where is Pearl?" I asked, noting the absence of the other sister. I'd never seen one without the other.

"She went back out mushroom hunting after I called you." She pointed a shaking hand toward her westside window. There was dirt under her nails. "That's where we found the pup. He was drinking water from a stream we have running through our back acres."

Parker took the little guy from me and felt along his ribs. As much as a human could, Parker growled, his anger deepening his words. "He looks like he hasn't eaten in a week."

Irritation colored Opal's wrinkled face. "I told you I fed him."

I could smell canned meat on the puppy's breath. It wasn't the most nutritious food for a growing dog, but he'd probably thought it was the best meal of his life. I put my hand on the elderly lady's rounded shoulder. "That was really kind of you, Opal. Thank you so much for calling us. We're happy you did."

My words appeased her. She smiled, the lines from the corners of her mouth to her outer nostrils deepening. "Will you let me know what happens to it?"

"We will." I reached out and gave her hand, the skin dry and loose, a gentle squeeze. "I promise."

"And tell that cousin of yours I said hello," the old lady added.

I grinned. Even though Buzz was my uncle, because we looked so close in age, we let the town believe we were cousins. "You can tell him yourself at breakfast."

As we walked back to the truck, Parker's anger rose from his skin like steam. It made me wish we'd have brought along Elvis, his trained service dog. "When we find the jerk who abandoned this pup, he's going to wish he was dead."

I tried to lighten the mood. "And what if it's a woman?"

He gave me a side-eye glance. "Same." At times, Parker opened like a fresh wound. Out of all his emotions, I think anger was the hardest for him to manage. Though love, I'm certain, was a close second.

"Maybe you should stay home when we find out who the owner is."

Parker raised a questioning brow.

"I'm already testifying at one trial. Any more, and I'm going to have to add witness for the prosecution to my resume."

Abruptly, Parker halted in his tracks. He turned to me, his face pinched for a moment, but quickly his expression relaxed. He laughed. "All right, Lily. I won't leave any bodies around for you to trip over."

"Thank the Goddess."

We continued to his truck. When he opened the back door, he gave me a strange look. "Is that really something?"

"What?"

"The Goddess." He gently placed the pup in the backseat kennel.

I swallowed at the lump in my throat and shrugged. "As much as anything is something."

I went around to the passenger side of the truck and got in. My heart thumped against the inside of my chest so hard I could hear the pounding waves in my ears. He hadn't asked me a single personal question about myself or my background since I'd shown him my fur. And no, that's not a euphemism. I'd partially shifted in front of him to let him get a good look at my true nature.

He hopped into the driver seat, closed the door behind him, and started the truck. He turned his curious blue-eyed gaze on me. "You know what I mean."

I swallowed again. "Actually, I'm not sure I do." I swiveled to face him. I tried to put compassion in my next words because I wasn't angry with Parker. I just really needed to know how far he wanted to take this conversation. "Is this small talk? Do you want a skim-the-surface answer, or do you really want to know? Because the last couple of months, I've gotten the impression you wish we could turn back time to a moment before you found out about me and keep it that way."

"I'm…" He gripped the steering wheel, his large arms flexing as his expression showed a myriad of conflict.

He wasn't ready. The thumping in my chest ceased with my disappointment and left a hollow ache in its place. "It's all right." I forced a smile that I worried looked more like a grimace. "We should get the dog back to the shelter." As if on cue, the puppy began to whimper.

Parker shook his head then gave a quick nod. Without another word, he put the truck in gear and got us on our way. I turned to the passenger window and focused on the landscape. Wildflowers, thickly leafed trees, rolling hills, and lush green grass made the spring one of the prettiest I'd ever seen. Unfortunately, my gaze kept diverting to the reflection in the window of Parker staring straight ahead, his lips thinned in concentration.

I had to accept the fact that he might never come around. Parker was a strong man who'd lived through his own hell during his short life. He understood trauma as well as I did. He watched many good friends, friends who had become like family, die in a war where everyone lost. I'd found my parents murdered, then seventeen years later, my brother was killed. They'd been the only family I'd ever known until seven months ago, when I'd traveled to Moonrise to meet Buzz, my father's brother, for the first time. I'd had a lot of hope for this new life, which is why it made me sad to think about moving back to Paradise Falls. I didn't want to go. Other than Haze Kinsey and her snarky familiar, Tizzy, I had nothing left there.

I glanced at Parker. I couldn't keep hurting him.

"I imagine if an alien spaceship landed on my lawn and little green men walked out, I'd have a hard time dealing with the harsh change in my reality." I tried to smile again, but it felt like the corners of my mouth were lifting fifty-pound weights. "I mean, I don't believe in little green men," I said, my voice soft. "But if one was put right in front of me, I guess I'd have to consider the possibility. And if aliens existed, what else in my world existed that I didn't know about? And I guess I'd worry about what I could trust and couldn't trust. Especially if those little green aliens could make themselves look like me. It would make me wonder about everyone I'd ever met."

The truck slowed as we approached the intersection of the highway leading back into town. Parker pulled off to the side of the road. For a millisecond, I worried he would tell me I could walk back to town.

Instead, he reached over and took my hand. "Would you like to come over for dinner tomorrow night?"

"I can't. Not tomorrow." I didn't really have any plans other than to wallow in self-pity. Tomorrow I would finally take my high school equivalency exam. It would start early in the morning and go all day. I should have just told Parker about the GED exam. The way the practice tests had gone for me, I was certain I would fail. I had science and math down, even history I could get a passing score, but English was the bane of my existence. I didn't want to spend the evening with Parker beating myself up over my inability to write decent essays.

Parker blinked. He hadn't expected to be turned down. "Sunday night then?"

The thumping in my chest returned as I realized he wasn't asking casually. I pivoted my gaze to meet his. "Are you inviting me as your friend? Or is this a date?"

He squeezed my hand, and I curled my fingers against his. He smiled. "Both. Or at least, I'd like it to be both."

I wanted to tell him about the GED test, but I didn't. Why was I so reluctant to tell him? I liked that he thought I was smart and educated, which I am, just not classically. I think deep down I worried that if he knew I was a high school dropout, it would change the way he looked at me. It was bad enough him finding out I wasn't altogether human.

"Okay." The pup in the back began to whine again.

"So, dinner Sunday?"

"Yes," I told him. "I've missed your spaghetti."

A shy smile graced his lips. "Then my plan is working."

CHAPTER FOUR

WHEN WE GOT BACK to the rescue center, Parker got the pup settled while I called Ryan Petry's office. His assistant, Marjorie, said their computer system was down, but she took the number from the puppy's tag and promised to call us as soon as she found out the owner information. Even so, Ryan would still need to check the dog out to make sure his only health issue was starvation.

Parker scowled when I mentioned Ryan's name. I knew he worried that Ryan was interested in me romantically, but nothing could be further from the truth.

Ryan was gay. Last I knew, he was still seeing Paul Simmons, the manager of Hayes Home Improvement Center. Paul was a handsome man, a little shorter than Ryan and a few years older, and they seemed to work. I couldn't tell Parker, though. The world I grew up in didn't place much value one way or another on sexuality. But this was not a Shifter-witch community. It was a small, rural

Midwest town, and while some, especially the younger generation, tended toward an open-mindedness, many of the older residents still had old-fashioned notions about what was and wasn't appropriate when it came to love and sex. So, until Ryan was ready to tell people, it wasn't my place to out him.

Near four o'clock, Addy Newton showed up for his shift wearing his letterman jacket, his blond hair cut short and his face freshly shaven. The teenage boy was the epitome of all-American. He came in to volunteer on Mondays, Wednesdays, and Fridays (now that football season was over) after school, and Sundays after church.

He'd been caught with chewing tobacco in his truck on school property, and because of that, he'd been suspended from playing baseball. His father had been furious, but I think getting kicked off the team relieved Addy. He wasn't a stupid guy, but his grades had slipped during football and basketball season.

"Hey, Lily. Parker," the teenager greeted us when he shuffled inside the office. He ran his fingers through his hair, so cool and confident. Right behind him was a teenage girl with dark hair, black skinny jeans, black ankle boots, and a black fitted sweater. Not so cool, and definitely not confident.

I smiled. It was Reggie's daughter, CeCe.

While CeCe was a bit gothy in style, I knew her black hair was natural. Her mother had the same raven mane. I also knew she was highly intelligent. She'd been tutoring Addy for the past two months to get him ready for final exams. The two of them looked like polar opposites, but it didn't take an enhanced set of senses to tell that Addy had a crush on the girl. CeCe, of course, was completely oblivious.

Parker nodded to Addy then gestured toward the door of the office. "I'm going to go check on the pup."

I waved at him then turned my attention to the teenagers. "Hey, you two. You both looking forward to graduation?"

"Sure," CeCe replied. It didn't set off alarms in my built-in lie detector, but her agreement wasn't quite the truth either.

I kept my focus on her. "I hear you're the salutatorian. Your mom sure is proud." I smiled. "Congratulations."

CeCe rolled her eyes but cracked a tiny smile that raised the color on her cheeks. "Thanks."

Addy nudged her shoulder with his. "Nerd."

I gave the man-boy a pointed look. "There are more effective ways of flirting, Addison."

Addy shook his head and blushed, but CeCe giggled, mostly because she thought I was kidding about him flirting. If he wanted to date CeCe, he was going to have to forego subtle. She was headed off to Washington University in St. Louis for the fall semester. If Addy didn't make his move soon, he'd lose his shot.

CeCe flashed me a quick smile. "I'm going to head home."

"I'll walk you out," Addy said.

I gave him a look that I hope said, "Go get that girl." He gave me a look back that said, "Mind your own business."

Ah, well. It would be his loss.

After they left, Parker came back into the room. He held our new ward in his arms. The dog's fur was damp, and the smell of mud and blood had been replaced by the medicinal smell of medicated shampoo. The little guy licked Parker's jaw like he was ice cream and Parker's smile made me swoon.

Goddess, that man made my ovaries ache. Seeing him with the puppy was like getting a glimpse of Parker as a dad. A flash of guilt pinched my gut. He deserved to experience all the joys that came with love. Marriage, children, growing old together. Two of the three he could never have with me.

I gestured toward the pup. "I see you gave him a bath."

"Yeah, he needed it." The dog stretched his neck up to lick Parker's jaw again.

"I'm glad he's not scared anymore."

"He ate three cups of puppy food. I had to stop him before he made himself sick."

Addy came back into the office. His eyes lit up when his gaze landed on our new ward. "What a cute little bruiser." He held out his arms. "Can I hold him?"

"Sure," Parker said. He handed over the damp bundle of fur to the teenager.

I watched as the puppy locked gazes with Addy. The kid's eyes softened, his jaw relaxed, and the corners of his mouth turned up in a wondrous smile.

"Uh oh," I said.

Parker crossed his arms. "What?"

"I recognize that look."

"Hey, there," Addy said. "I can't believe how much you look like Smooshie, minus a hundred pounds."

"Hey," I said in defense of my dog. "She's only eighty pounds."

Addy laughed and tickled the pup's belly, laughing again as he got whacked in the face with a tail.

Addy looked up at me, his expression almost dazed. "What's his name?"

"We don't know, yet." I heard the front door ding.

"Lily? Parker? You all back here?" Ryan Petry asked.

I noted the scowl on Parker's face that he quickly tried to hide.

"Hey, Ryan," I said loudly. "We're back in the office."

He rounded the corner, his dark brown hair perfectly styled, and wearing a crisply pressed pair of black slacks and a blue and green striped button-down shirt that made his emerald-green eyes appear even more jewel-like. He really was a handsome man. He flashed me his trademark smile, patted the inside door frame, and said, "What's cookin' good lookin'?"

I tried not to giggle.

"What can we do for you, Petry?" Parker asked.

Ryan raised his brow. I'm pretty sure he knew Parker was jealous, and it didn't help that he did nothing to alleviate Parker's feelings that he was trying to court me.

"I have the information on that owner you were asking about. The owner's name is Donnie Doyle."

"Who?" Parker asked.

I recognized the name right away—the waiter from Dally's Tavern. Parker had been in there several times since Donnie started working there. I was surprised he didn't know the name.

"He's an adjunct at Two Hills Community College in the computer department. He's teaching an introductory course while working on his graduate degree at the university." Ryan shrugged. "He seems like a nice guy. I can't believe he'd abandon Tino."

"Tino?" Addy said. "That's a weird name."

"Short for Valentino," Ryan said. "The great lover," he added when Addy's expression remained oblivious. "Anyhow, he seemed pretty devoted to the dog when he brought him in for a wellness exam and vaccinations a month ago."

"The state we found this dog in is inexcusable," Parker said, a simmer of anger in his voice.

Ryan frowned, his silky brown hair curtaining his eyes. He walked to where Addy stood and ran his slender fingers over the puppy's body. "He's definitely emaciated."

"He's starved," Parker corrected.

"Abandonment is a class-C misdemeanor." Ryan shook his head. "We can have him cited, but the most he'll incur is a fine."

"Or I could kick his teeth down his throat and assure him if he ever takes in an animal again, he'll be in the market for a second set of dentures."

Ryan raised a brow at Parker. "Calm down. I understand you're upset but getting mad isn't going to help. We need to call the sheriff's department and see if we can get this incident officially investigated."

"You think I should calm down?" Parker said in a quiet, scary voice. He took a stalking step toward Ryan.

I stood up and put myself between them. "Do you think they will charge him?" I asked Ryan.

"I'm not sure." He kept his eye on Parker but made no move to back down. They'd been high school buddies, so Ryan was used to Parker's moods. "The sheriff's department should charge him, but in these rural areas, sometimes animal abuses are overlooked."

"Tell me about it," Parker said, his large, expressive hands flexed at his sides. I knew he was thinking about a puppy mill he'd tried to shut down a month ago. He couldn't get animal control to do more than give the operation a warning. At least his anger had shifted away from Ryan.

I raised my hand to get the men's attention. "Why don't we go and ask the guy about Tino? Have our own investigation."

"That's not a good idea, Lily," Ryan said.

"Why not? How dangerous could he be?" From what I'd seen, the guy was more a lover than a fighter.

"Let's call Nadine," Parker said.

I frowned but nodded my acquiescence. Nadine Booth had issued Donnie a speeding ticket, so at least she knew him. "That's a good idea, Parker."

He grinned. "I get them from time to time."

Ryan pulled out his cell phone. "I'll call her."

"Do you need her phone number?" I asked.

"No." Ryan shook his head. "I have it." He pushed a button on his phone. Parker and I waited. I heard it ring, then I heard Nadine on the other end say, "Ryan. To what do I owe the honor of this call?" Humor lit up her every word.

"Hey, Nadine. I'm down at the Moonrise Pit Bull Rescue with an abandoned pup. I was wondering if you might go check on the owner."

"What do you suspect?" she asked, her tone more serious.

"Possibly willful abandonment. I know the guy though, from the college. I find it hard to believe."

"All right. I'll check on him. Address?"

Ryan said, "Forty-one Northeast Seven Hundred Road."

She'd said the other night that Donnie lived close to me, but I noted the address for good measure. Seven Hundred Road was about a mile from my place. I loved living rurally. It was especially good for

Smooshie. I had ten acres full of trees, which made it a great place to run free.

Ryan ended the call. "Nadine says she'll stop by Doyle's place before her shift ends."

I nodded like he was giving me new information. Ryan, like everyone else in Moonrise, aside from my uncle and Parker, had no idea that all my senses were superhuman. Since Parker had found out about me, or rather, since I'd forced a reveal on him, I'd been avoiding any long conversations with Buzz. He'd been pretty unhappy with me about revealing myself to Parker.

"Lily?"

I blinked. Parker gave me a strange questioning look. "Are you okay?"

"Yes," I said. "Why?"

"You just had a far-off look on your face."

Addy put the puppy down, and Tino ran over to me and perched between my knees.

Ryan chuckled. "Someone has a crush on you."

I perked up my left eyebrow, automatically reaching down to stroke Tino between his floppy little ears. "I have that effect."

"Yeah, you do," Parker said. When I met his gaze, he added, "On dogs, I mean." A red blush crept up his neck toward his ears. The honey scent of him hung heavy in the air.

"I'll take Tino out and play with him a little if that's okay," Addy said, oblivious to Parker's discomfort.

"Good idea," Parker said. "I'm going to check on Elvis. He probably needs to be let out too." Plus, after the day we'd had, he probably needed some Elvis time to calm his nerves.

"And I better check in at the clinic," Ryan said.

On cue, I added, "I better go get Smooshie. She's probably driving your dad nuts."

Parker chuckled. "He loves her."

I smiled at him. "She's easy to love."

Parker shook his head. "I'm not sure Elvis would agree."

I waved my hand, grabbed my purse, and stood up. "There is no accounting for taste."

*****

Greer had closed The Rusty Wrench for the day. I found him and Smooshie playing a vigorous game of tug-o-war in the living room of his Victorian home. His wife had decorated when she'd been alive, and in the past ten years, he hadn't changed a single item except for what could only be described as a small shrine he'd made to her over the fireplace mantel.

Smooshie dropped her end of the rope and skittered happily across the hardwood floor, sliding on the pads of her large paws, her nails clicking as she danced around me in greeting. I knelt beside her and wrapped my arms around her neck.

"Hey, girl. I missed you." I looked past her to Greer. "Thanks for watching the wrecking ball for me."

He smiled, his eyes crinkling at the corners. "Anytime, Lily."

The older mechanic was handsome with his thick graying hair and extra lines in his forehead and around his blue eyes. He was the epitome of aging well. I couldn't help but wonder if Parker would look like him as he grew older.

I noticed Greer had shaved the scruff from his face. Unusual for him, especially in the evenings. And he smelled like musk and alcohol. Cologne? I understood showering after a long day of working on cars, but why was Greer wearing cologne?

CHAPTER FIVE

"HEY, SMOOSH. DID YOU have fun with your play date?" I kept my left hand on the wheel of old Martha and reached over with my right to pat Smooshie's broad head. She kicked her nose up and licked my hand. "I don't think Greer showered and shaved for you, girlfriend. I wish I could speak dog because I have a feeling if anyone knows who he spiffed up for, it's you."

I hadn't planned on going anywhere but straight home, but then I saw the small white marker for 700 Road on the left.

Don't turn. Don't turn. Don't turn, I told myself. After all, Nadine would be investigating. I should definitely stay out of it, right? Just because I'd talked to Donnie a few times at a bar didn't mean I knew him well enough to stop by his home. Besides, I didn't move to Moonrise to be an investigator.

And yet, my instincts were pinging hardcore. Plus, cats were curious creatures. In other words, it was in my nature to snoop.

I glanced at Smoosh. "It won't hurt to drive past his house, right? No stopping."

Smooshie cocked her ears back and forth. I took that as an agreement.

Less than a mile down the gravel road, I saw a mailbox surrounded by a cluster of tiger lilies, bright orange at the top of tall green leaves, with *41 NE 700* written on the side. This was the place. I stopped the truck in the middle of the road.

"I know," I told Smoosh. "I said I wouldn't stop. But I'm not getting out of the truck. I'm observing." I wanted to see where Tino came from. Doyle's place was a red brick ranch-style house with white decorative shutters. There was an ornamental windmill in the middle of a circular flower bed in the front yard. The walkway to the door was lined with purple bearded irises. It seemed a little "retirement home" for such a young guy, but it was nice.

I let my foot up off the brake and rolled the truck forward then pulled off to the side of the road.

Smooshie stood up, excitement and energy vibrating her body. She was aching for an adventure. "You're a bad influence, girl." As if she had to encourage me to snoop.

I clenched the steering wheel and debated the merits of walking up to Doyle's front door and knocking. How dangerous could a man who owned an ornamental windmill be?

I grabbed Smooshie's leash from the dash and clipped her in. Having her around tended to diffuse most tense situations. Besides, I could take care of myself.

The grass was about a week overdue for a trim, reminding me that I needed to figure out how to scrape enough money together to buy a push mower to care for my lawn. My yard was really big, and every estimate I'd received from lawn services was over two-hundred dollars to mow, trim, and weed whack. Buying a push mower and a gas-powered string trimmer would save me a lot of money. Besides, I'd always found yard work relaxing.

Smooshie yanked the leash, pulling me onto the grass so she could squat down and pee. She sniffed the ground hard, darting her head back and forth with purpose, on the scent of something I couldn't yet detect. My sense of smell was good, but not on par with a dog whose sense of smell was thousands of times better.

I crouched down and plucked at the grass where Smooshie had buried her nose. Iron. My mouth watered. Old blood. I felt ill as I tugged on the leash and made my way toward the door.

The faint scent of decomposing flesh chilled me, not because it was super strong, but because it was present at all. Why had I turned left, for goddess' sake?

The blood alone wasn't a huge deal, but there was no escaping what that other smell meant. Something or someone was dead in the house.

Smooshie lunged at the door, and I pulled her back. "We can't go in." I dug into my purse to find my phone. Nadine needed to investigate Doyle now, not later.

I pulled it out just as Smooshie yanked again, her instinct overriding her manners, and my cell phone ripped from my hand and dropped onto the concrete sidewalk.

The cracking noise when it hit startled my excited pittie long enough for me to rein her in so I could pick it up.

The blackened screen looked like a spider went to town on a crazy, densely threaded web.

"Shoot."

Smooshie looked up at me, her wide face split in a grin, tongue lolling out the side while she panted eagerly.

"No," I told her. "We're not going in the house, so you can wipe that smile right off your face, young lady."

Smooshie hopped up and pawed at the air in front of me before settling down on all fours again, her tail stirring up a breeze like an accordion-fold fan.

"Nope," I said. However, my phone was trashed, and it was either go in and find Doyle's phone to call Nadine or drive all the way back to town. But what if someone was hurt inside? I would feel awful if I could have helped an injured person and didn't.

Oh, who was I kidding? There was nothing alive in that house. That stench could only come from something dead.

A phone rang, and I nearly jumped out of my skin.

"Holy smokes," I whispered as my pulse fluttered in my neck. The phone rang again. And again. I could go in and answer it. After, I'd use that phone to call Nadine.

It was a plan. Not a great plan, but a plan all the same. I wrapped the dog's leash around my hand multiple times, reeling her into my side. I took my training clicker from my pocket as added backup. "You behave. Whatever we find in there."

The screen door was unlocked and the latch broken. The main door was ajar. The scent of death, lemon, and pine—a caustic combination—inundated my senses. I held my breath.

Smooshie jerked me forward. I pulled her back. Maybe I should drive back to town, I thought, as I turned the corner just inside the door to the kitchen.

Donnie Doyle lay on his stomach on the floor, his head turned to the right toward me, which made it easy to identify him. Blood had dripped down from a gash on the side of his head to the crown of his forehead, darkening his brows. His head was surrounded by dried blood, but I didn't see any blood anywhere else. There was a smear of oil by his bare feet, and the bottom of his left foot was glistening.

An accident? Maybe. But the brownish-red stain on his cheeks and hands threw me off. I'd never seen anything like it, not even in all the medical books I'd read. A small amount of white stuff, maybe spittle, crusted at the corner of his mouth.

I looked around the room. I didn't see anything that would cause any of the damage I was seeing. Had he had a seizure and hit his head when he fell?

I detected the reek of putrefaction, all signs of the body digesting itself. Donnie Doyle had been dead for a week, at least. I had to suppress my revulsion as the full force of pungent decay overwhelmed me. It was as if rotten eggs dipped in ammonia had taken a bath in a sulfur spring multiplied by ten.

Smooshie began to whine, her body hugging tightly against my leg.

"I know, girl. I don't like it either." I scanned the counters for a phone but didn't see one. However, I did see blood on the corner of a white marble-topped center island. From across the room, I could see a clear glass turned upside down in the sink, but there was nothing else in there or on the counters, not even crumbs. I wanted to go in and investigate further, but I didn't want the sheriff arresting me for contaminating the crime scene more.

"Let's go look in the other rooms," I told Smooshie.

I held my breath until I reached the living room. It was immaculate. Hardwood floors with a high polish, lint-free furniture, dust-free end tables, coffee tables, and bookshelves. Even his television was spotless, no fingerprints or smudges. The dust-free part was a huge feat, considering Donnie lived on a rural road. The smell of lemon and pine became more potent as I traversed the room. If he had a phone in the living room, though, I didn't see it.

The first door in the hallway was open. Inside, a neatly made queen-size bed with a green comforter had been placed against the far wall. There was a dark mahogany bedside table, a bookshelf, and a matching dresser. Other than that, the room lacked any personal touches, except for a clock on the wall in the shape of a sundial and some modern art prints that filled in the space around it. Was this where a twenty-four-year-old male graduate student slept?

Donnie struck me as the kind of guy who lived more adventurously.

Smooshie growled. She crouched down, her ears going back. Her normally friendly brown eyes were narrowed and alert.

"Shhhh," I said quietly, giving her a reassuring pat on the head. "Let me listen." I let my cougar slip forward. A small shift, just enough to turn my nails into claws and sharpen my eyes, ears, and nose.

I heard it, then, a whirring noise coming from down the hall. It sounded like a computer hard drive fan. I stepped toward the noise, and Smooshie's nails clicked along the hardwood. I pulled back my animal side just in case someone alive was still in the house. I'd already broken Buzz's rule about showing my true self to a human once, I wouldn't make that mistake again.

The whir came from behind a closed door down the hall from the bathroom, another immaculately clean room. Slowly, I opened the door.

Brrrrriiiiiinnnng!

I squawked, and Smooshie started barking. The room was an office. There were a couple of black metal file cabinets, a utilitarian desk, a fire safe, a computer, and a landline phone.

I blinked as it rang again. I crossed the floor to the desk and picked up the phone. "Hello?"

"Hi." The voice sounded surprised on the other end. "This is Michelle Floyd, human resources manager for Two Hills Community College. I'm calling for Donald Doyle. Do I have the right number?"

"Yes, ma'am. This is Mr. Doyle's phone number."

"Can I speak to him?" Her voice was suddenly tart and sharp.

"I'm afraid you can't right now." I didn't know what to say to the woman. It wasn't my place to tell people Donnie was dead.

Her tone became even terser. "You tell Mr. Doyle that he's missed a week of classes. It's completely unacceptable. He needs to call me immediately."

"If I speak to him, I'll let him know." I hung up. I felt a little shaky. I needed to call Nadine, but without my cell phone, I didn't have her number. Heck, I didn't have anyone's number, and I hadn't bothered to memorize my contacts. Which meant...

I punched in the three numbers I dreaded dialing most. Nine. One. One.

"Can I get your name?" an operator asked.

I thought about lying and leaving before the cops arrived, but I didn't. Instead, I sighed and said, "Lily Mason."

"And what's your emergency, Lily?"

"I found a dead body," I told her. "Again."

CHAPTER SIX

SHERIFF AVERY, A BURLY man with short, graying brown hair, glared at me from the porch. He'd insisted that Smooshie and I wait by my truck until he could question me further. He shoved his hands in his pockets as he talked to Deputy Bobby Morris, a tall black man with intense brown eyes. I'd learned from Nadine that Bobby had two boys under the age of ten with his wife of thirteen years. He had been a state trooper before taking the job at the sheriff's department. I liked Bobby, and I hoped the sheriff would send him over to take my statement.

Bobby flashed me a sympathetic look before he went back inside the house. Nope. The sheriff was going to interrogate…er…question me himself.

I braced myself as he walked toward me with a menacing stride.

"Young lady, why am I not surprised to find you in the middle of, yet again, another death in this county?"

"I guess I'm just really lucky, Sheriff." I placed my hand on my hip. Smooshie, who I'd put in the truck, stuck her head out the window I'd rolled halfway down and growled. "Hush, girl." My soul puppy was reacting to my emotional state. I tried to relax. "I can assure you that I don't like finding dead bodies any more than you *like* me finding them."

"Uh huh." He pursed his lips, the line between his brows deepening with his frown. "What is your relationship to Donnie Doyle?"

"I don't have one."

He raised a questioning brow. "Are you certain? Doyle has a reputation for ladies, and you do frequent the bar where he works."

"Are you keeping tabs on me, Sheriff?"

We stared at each other for several tense seconds until Avery blinked. "It's a small town, Ms. Mason. People talk."

"Well, they certainly weren't talking about Donnie and me."

The sheriff's expression soured even more, if possible. "Then why are you here?"

"Someone called in a lost dog to the shelter. A puppy. He'd been half-starved, and we found out from the vet he belongs to Doyle."

"Why didn't you call the sheriff's department to investigate?"

"I did."

"We don't have a log of your phone call?"

"Well, we called..." Crap. Would I be getting Nadine in trouble if I said Ryan had called her directly? The fact that she dated my uncle and the two of us were friends seemed to be two strikes against her in Avery's eyes.

"Yes?" The sheriff furrowed his bushy brows. "You called who?"

"I called nine-one-one as soon as I could."

"Uh huh," he muttered. "Tell me again why you unlawfully entered the property."

I had to fight the impulse to roll my eyes. Sheriff Avery disliked me enough to haul me into his office if he got a bug up his butt about my attitude. I needed to stay calm.

"I door was ajar, and I wanted to make sure no one was hurt inside. Especially when I saw the door was open."

"And why didn't you call for help as soon as you saw the blood?"

I pulled my shattered phone from my purse. "I had no way of getting ahold of you guys without going inside. The phone in the house was ringing, and I thought the quickest way to get help if Doyle was injured was to find it."

"Did you remove anything from the house?"

"Do you want to frisk me?"

Avery's puffy face turned red. "Don't push it, Ms. Mason."

"No," I told him, "I didn't remove anything. Other than using the phone, I was careful not to touch anything."

"And what about your mutt?"

A crackling sizzle of protectiveness zipped through me at his disdain for Smooshie. "She's not a mutt." I closed my eyes for a second, hoping the color hadn't changed to reflect my inner cougar.

When I opened them, the corner of Avery's mouth tugged up in a half-smile. "You gonna answer the question?"

A white luxury car pulled in behind my truck, distracting the sheriff long enough for me to get myself centered again. Reggie Crawford got out from the driver's side. She wore a violet wrap dress and some killer black heels. "Someone call for a coroner?" She smiled at me. "Oh, hey, Lily. Why are you here?"

The sheriff scowled.

I shook my head, but said, "I just have that kind of luck." Now that she was closer, I noticed she'd had her hair and nails done to a T. Pre-graduation prep, probably. Reggie was really freaked out about her ex's impending arrival.

"You look great," I told her. She smelled brightly of citrus and raspberries. "And that perfume is yummy." There was the undercurrent of another scent, something spicy and familiar, but I couldn't quite place it.

"Thanks, Lily." Reggie smiled brightly. "Now, Sheriff Avery. About that body?"

The sheriff's lip curled in a snarl. "It's a simple case of accidental death, Dr. Crawford. Victim slipped on his kitchen floor and hit his head on the corner of his center island."

"Not that I don't trust your medical opinion, Sheriff, but I wouldn't be doing my duty as coroner for this county if I didn't at least go take a peek. Do we know who it is, yet?"

"It's Donnie Doyle," I told her.

Reggie blanched then regained her composure. "The waiter?"

Before I could confirm, Sheriff Avery stepped between us and gave me a look that told me to shut up or else. I held up my hands and took a step back toward my truck, trying to make a strategic retreat.

His lips thinned as he glared at me. "Stay put, Ms. Mason." He turned to Reggie then and made a swooping gesture toward the house with his left arm. "Body is in the kitchen."

Deputy Morris handed Reggie some paper booties for her feet when she reached the front door.

She slipped her heels off on the small porch and placed the covers over her bare feet. Dang, Reggie had nice legs. And considering the paramedics, Morris, and even the sheriff had cast quick but appreciative glances, I wasn't the only one who noticed. She had nothing, and I mean nothing, to worry about when her ex-husband came to town.

I cleared my throat. The sheriff's ears and cheeks reddened. "Look. If you need to ask me any more questions, you know where I work and you know where I live. I won't be hard to find." I was going to have to stop by Walmart and see about getting another phone. "Can I go? I need to get Smooshie home and fed." On cue, my girl began to whine. Loudly.

"Fine," Avery said. "I'll be talking to you later." He sounded like my high school principal, Mr. Roderick Stark. A warlock with bad breath and an even worse temper. The man was always blustering about one thing or another. My bestie Haze Kinsey and I were always on his short list.

I gave my nemesis a perky smile. "It's been nice seeing you again, Sheriff Avery." I nodded my head and walked quickly to the driver-side door of old Martha. I jumped in the truck and started it up before the sheriff changed his mind. I could tell by the look on his face, he would have preferred to haul me away in handcuffs before letting me go.

I wanted to call Parker or Nadine. I really needed to get ahold of Nadine to warn her. The sheriff might be a jerk, but he wasn't stupid, and I didn't want her facing backlash at work over our friendship. Neither Parker nor Nadine was going to get a call from me, though. Not without a phone.

Instead of turning left out on the highway, I took a right. I couldn't leave Nadine in the lurch about Doyle. Since I didn't know where she was, I headed straight to The Cat's Meow, my uncle Buzz's diner.

It was dinnertime on a Friday night. The crowd at the diner usually started at five and didn't slow down until nine. Buzz liked it busy. He said hard work kept him young. Of course, since he was a werecougar like myself, he really didn't need any help in the "staying young" department. He and Nadine had been living together for three months, so I knew he'd have her on speed dial.

Cars and trucks lined the small parking lot outside the restaurant. I parked a block down on the street and walked back up. It took a few minutes because Smooshie had to stop every ten steps to pee.

I didn't blame her. It had been several hours since the last time I'd gone to the bathroom, and the cola I'd consumed at the end of my shift was painfully stretching my bladder.

I walked with my knees pressed together as I closed in on the last few feet to the diner. I quickened my pace, but unfortunately, my nemesis—not the sheriff, the other one, Naomi Wells, with her golden-blonde hair and rosy complexion—barred my entry.

"Fantastic," I muttered. Naomi was a reporter for a large St. Louis newspaper, a real "hometown girl makes good" story, and for some reason, she'd decided I was a story worth pursuing. She'd been best friends with Parker's high school sweetheart, Bridgette Jones.

Bridgette, who turned out to be a murderer, killed herself after she shot me. Her husband, Tom, tried to finish the job. Naomi had written several stories about the killings, painting both Bridgette and Tom as misunderstood. She'd been trying to get an interview with me for two months. Back in March, she'd tried to get to me through Parker. As his date. That still burned my butt.

"Why, if it isn't Lily Mason?" She smiled. "Just the gal I was looking for."

Smooshie shoved her head between Naomi's legs and under her red A-line skirt. Naomi yelped and pushed her skirt down.

I pulled Smooshie back. "Stop that," I said to her. "You never know what evil you might find lurking in dark corners."

She glared and gave me a flat smile. "Why don't you ask Parker?" She winked. "He has the inside scoop."

Wow. Ouch. She'd made a quick precision strike, and it cut deep. Deeper than I wanted to admit. I knew they'd gone out on a date back in March, but Parker had assured me he wasn't interested in

Naomi. She wasn't pinging my lie detector, at least not completely, but I suspected my magic was a little broken when it came to all things Parker.

"What do you want, Naomi?" I crossed my legs and bounced on my toes to keep from peeing my pants.

"Are you having a seizure?"

"Only when you're around." Smooshie, who usually tried to drag me around, decided to sit quietly and watch the cat fight. I hated to disappoint her, but if I didn't get inside, I was going to have to explain the humiliating puddle at my feet. "You need to get out of my way."

Naomi towered over me by seven inches, so I'm sure it surprised her when I gave her a light shove that sent her staggering sideways. I tugged at Smoosh, who was slow on the uptake that we were moving on and powered my way through the door.

The booths and tables were mostly occupied. I drew a few stares from some of the locals, including Dalton Newton, Addy's father, and his wife, Jessica. When I met Dalton's eyes, he looked away. I'd killed his brother Nick, not that anyone knew, though. Except for Parker, of course. Parker told the police it had been a large animal attack, which hadn't been a complete lie. I'd shifted into my *other* nature to save Parker's life when Nick tried to shoot him. In the process, I'd torn out Nick's throat.

I wish I felt more remorse. Nick was human. I should have felt bad, but when a guy tries to kill you and the man you might be in love with, it's hard to feel anything but relief when he's gone. Besides, if I had to go to a murder trial, I'd rather go as a witness than a defendant.

I knew from Addy that Dalton didn't blame me for what happened to his brother. Still, I think I served as an embarrassing reminder of something he wanted to forget.

Freda delivered a tray of burgers and fried tenderloins to a four-top. She acknowledged me with a curt nod as I took Smooshie through the arch past the bathrooms and toward Buzz's office. I ushered her inside the small room.

"Behave." I pointed at her then ruffled her ear while shifting back and forth on the balls of my feet pee-pee-dance style. "I'll be right back."

She gave me a cockeyed look, a big grin splitting her wide jaw.

"You heard me." I backed up and closed the door between us before dashing the few feet up the hall to the ladies' room. After peeing for what seemed like an hour, I washed my hands and cussed a little because the rack above the sink was out of paper towels.

The door handle rattled.

"Occupied," I said. I ripped a long strip of toilet paper off the wall-mounted roll and began patting it between my wet palm. Little pieces of the white fall-apart paper were sticking to my skin.

"Christ, I've got to go," I heard a woman say in a quiet voice. Thanks to my Shifter hearing, it came through loud and clear.

Another woman said, "As long as she's been in there, you better hope there's some air freshener."

"You don't think?" asked the first woman. "Ew."

While I hadn't had to poop, I thought it was hideously inappropriate for the two women to be whispering about the possibility. I grabbed another piece of toilet paper, unlocked the door, and flung it open. Both woman, one in her mid-thirties with mousy brown hair and the other a middle-aged brunette with glasses, widened their eyes in surprise.

"All yours," I said. I gave them a pointed look before heading to the kitchen. First priority, after not peeing my pants, was to get Nadine on the phone.

Buzz stood near the grill, meat sizzling and his spatula in hand. He wore his mop of coppery red hair under a ball cap, and he kept his beard and mustache trimmed neat. My uncle, who was in his seventies, looked to be in his late twenties-early thirties. He and Nadine had dated for eight months before they decided to move in together. He'd warned me off forming attachments to humans, but as he could plainly attest, talking about it and doing it where two different things.

"Hey, Lily." Buzz smiled when he saw me. "Did you come in for dinner?" He flipped five burgers then buttered some buns and threw them on the empty side of the grill.

"I need to talk to Nadine."

"She's still at work. Did you try calling her?"

I retrieved my broken phone from my purse and showed him the shattered screen. "Oops." I shook my head. "I found a dead body."

Buzz winced. "Another one?"

"Believe me, I'd stop if I could. I think I might have gotten Nadine in trouble with the sheriff. I want to warn her."

He wiped his hands on a white towel poking out of his apron pocket. He walked across the room to a shelf and grabbed his cell phone, an old-fashioned flip phone.

"Dang, you really are old. When did you get that dinosaur? You trying to party like it's nineteen ninety-nine?"

"Ha ha. I got this back in two-thousand and ten, and it's never given me any trouble. It's reliable and, unlike your phone, virtually indestructible. I can't tell you how many times I've dropped this thing, and it will still make crystal-clear calls."

He had a point. People with glass screens should not throw stones. "Oh, just give me old reliable." I flipped it open.

"She's speed-dial one," Buzz said.

"That's so sweet." I grinned, pushed the asterisk and then the one. The phone rang after a brief pause.

On the second ring, Nadine picked up. "I can't talk now, babe. I'm in a world of crap at work right now."

"I'm sorry, babe," I said. "I think it might be my fault."

"I thought you were Buzz. I'm at the Doyle house right now with the crime scene techs."

"Is the sheriff still there?"

"He stayed long enough to chew me a second a-hole."

"I feel awful about that," I said.

"Oh, don't. It's not like he can fire me because we're friends." She didn't add, "even if he wanted to," but she didn't need to say it. It was evident the sheriff had a major problem with me.

"Did you find anything in the house?"

"Nothing that we didn't expect. It looks like a straightforward accident. He slipped on some cooking oil, hit his head on the corner of his center island, and that was that."

The scenario seemed plausible, only… "Where's the oil bottle? I didn't see it when I was in there."

"I… I'm not sure." She paused, but I could hear the slow inhalation and exhalation of breath. "It's in the cabinet."

"Does it make sense to you that he would spill oil on the ground then put the bottle away before he cleaned it up? And what was he using the oil for? It just doesn't feel…authentic." I let the thought hang there.

"I'll keep looking here," Nadine said. "I don't expect to find anything, but I've learned not to ignore your instincts. But just for clarification, what do you think happened?"

"I've got no big theories."

"I'll take a small one. Give it up, Lils."

I sighed. "Doesn't the house seem a little neat to you? Everything in its place. He lives out on a gravel road, and I didn't see a speck of dust, and considering he's been dead for at least a week…"

"You think someone came in and cleaned up?"

"No. Maybe. The way his items were placed around the house, I get the feeling the guy was pretty OCD."

"Yeah, I can see that being his thing. It is weirdly neat in here."

"Check his office. It wasn't nearly as pristine as the areas where a guest might frequent. Except for the cup in the sink."

I could hear the light tread of her footsteps. "The cup is washed. That doesn't seem that unusual."

"If this guy is an 'everything has its place and everything in its place' kind of guy, why would he leave a washed cup in the sink? Doesn't it seem more likely he would have put it away?"

"Hmmm. Maybe." In the background, I heard a man call for Nadine. "I've got to go," she said. "I'll call you later." She hung up before I could tell her that I didn't have a working phone.

Buzz had been cooking during my conversation with Nadine, but I knew he'd overheard the entire conversation. "I don't suppose I could talk you into staying out of this, whatever it turns out to be?"

"Sure," I said. "You can always give it a go." It wouldn't take much to keep me out of it. I'd moved to Moonrise to get away from death and mayhem, but it seemed to follow me around like a stalker.

He chuckled and gave me a curious look. "Are you okay?"

"As opposed to…?"

"Not okay?" He shrugged. "You've been kind of mopey since all that trouble happened in March."

"I don't want to talk about it."

His expression softened around his eyes. "I know I was rough on you after it all went down, but I really do understand. If someone was attacking Nadine, I might do the same."

"I still don't want to talk about it." It was nice to know he did care enough about Nadine to risk exposure. Really, I wished he'd tell her the truth about us. More for selfish reasons than anything romantic. I hated lying to my friend. However, telling her would expose Buzz too. I would never do that to him.

The aroma of smoke gave me the perfect diversion. I pointed to the grill. "I think something's burning."

CHAPTER SEVEN

I DROVE STRAIGHT HOME from the diner. I parked in front of the small white trailer next to my house. The trailer was my actual home right now. My two-story farmhouse, a work in progress, sat on ten acres of wooded land. It was going to be early fall before the house would be livable, especially since I was on a budget. The reward for finding the bank's stolen money had paid off the mortgage, which suited me fine, but there wasn't anything left over for actual repairs.

The best part of owning my own forest was the thick tree cover that gave Smooshie and me ample privacy to stretch our furry legs. Out here in the middle of nowhere, I could change into my cougar form and explore every inch of the back property with my pretty pittie.

In the morning, I'd head to Walmart for a new cell phone, but tonight, I wanted to run. Smooshie leaped out of the truck when I opened the passenger door. She turned around, her tail stirring the air as she playfully barked a sort of "roo roo roo rooo." My big girl had a way of sensing when I planned an evening dressed in fur, claws, and sharp teeth.

Smooshie always got excited when I started to undress, even when a nightly run wasn't in the plan. I'd had to take to changing for work or a night out behind closed doors so she wouldn't put herself in a happy frenzy. Besides, I couldn't take the disappointment in her eyes during those times when she would realize we weren't going for a run. Tonight, however, my girl would get to really stretch her legs.

Finding the body, running into Naomi, her intimations that her and Parker had sex, all of it made my skin itch. I yanked my T-shirt over my head as Smooshie followed me to the trailer. I took off my bra next. At the steps, I opened the door, unzipped my ankle boots, and chucked them inside, along with my other discarded clothes. Smoosh trotted around, prancing with energy.

When I shimmied out of my pants and undies, I gave Smooshie a big smile. "Time to run, baby girl."

My cougar prowled around inside me. She was almost as excited as the pit bull. I willed her to the surface, embracing the warmth of fur as it sprouted along my skin. The bones in my body cracked and reshaped until I transformed into my animal form. It took mere seconds and, as always, felt like unmitigated bliss. I loved the feel of my claws gripping the grass as we ran into the woods. I found my favorite tree, a great oak with thick branches the size of Parker's thighs that I could climb up on and perch.

From my roost, I saw headlights coming up the road. I recognized the sound of the engine and the crunch of the heavy tires rolling over the gravel. It was Parker's dually pickup. I jumped down from the tree, landing on the grass with the light ease of my kind. I didn't want to see Parker right now, not after my run-in with Naomi at The Cat's Meow. That woman certainly knew how to push my buttons.

The truck pulled up to the trailer. The engine stopped before the headlamps went out. I wanted to run away. It wasn't exactly a mature way to behave, but it was better than my first impulse, which was to go all crazy cougar on his butt. I didn't have the right to hold his past intimacies against him, but Naomi Wells?

I tried not to dwell on the fact that I was the one who had encouraged him to go out with her in the first place.

When Parker got out of the truck, I hid behind a tree. I know, really mature. I wasn't sure if seeing me in my cougar form would freak him out more, especially since we hadn't really talked about it since the first time. You know, when I went all Rick Grimes and bit a man's throat out. I shook my head. Damn Uncle Buzz for getting me hooked on *The Walking Dead*. I'd marathoned all of the early seasons in less than a month.

Changing into human form didn't seem like a good option either. I mean, I didn't relish the idea of trotting up to the trailer completely naked to greet him. Smooshie sat down next to me, her tail whacking slowly against my hind quarter as she whined. I guess she couldn't understand why we weren't happy to see Parker. I hissed through my fangs and rubbed my shoulder against the dog. She needed to keep quiet. I didn't want Parker to know I was out here.

The trailer porch light, the one near the front door, illuminated Parker as he knocked. "Lily?" I heard him ask. He knocked again then stepped off the bottom stair.

Goddess, why did that man have to look so good? What could I possibly say to him right now that wouldn't screw things up between us? He'd finally made the first move, and I worried that if he saw me in werecougar form again, it would freak him out, and he'd never want anything to do with me again.

So, since I wasn't ready to push my Shifter luck with Parker, I made like a scaredy-cougar and ran to the back of the property with Smooshie hot on my heels. She barked at our spirited run. If I'd been capable of a fully-furred wince, I would have. There was no way Parker hadn't heard her. So much for a stealthy getaway.

Once we made it to the edge of my woods, I knew Donnie Doyle's house was only a couple miles up the road. Investigating on my own was such a bad idea, but it gave me a legitimate reason to avoid my personal drama.

I heard my name bellowed in the distance. Parker was searching for me, but I didn't want to be found. Stretching my strides to increase my speed, Smooshie by my side, we made our way to the Doyle property. I approached cautiously, making sure there wasn't any police or any other human presence around. The house was dark. I didn't see a single light on, and there were no cars or other vehicles in the driveway.

Inhaling deeply, I tasted the air. The earlier acrid smell of death had faded. Smooshie, who was easily distracted, shoved her nose into a nearby clump of grass. More than likely she caught the scent of a mole or a raccoon. Doyle's rental sat on a wide-open plot. He had two trees, a knotty redbud on the side of the house and a large silver maple in the backyard.

I tried to catch the scent of something that wasn't a small critter but couldn't detect any human activity other than what the police and crime scene technicians might've left behind. It was stupid to think that after all this time, and with as many people who had been traipsing in and out of the house since I'd called 9-1-1, that I might find some important clue. If there was even a clue to be found.

I scouted the perimeter of the house until I reached the office window. I could still hear the whir of Doyle's computer. I guess no one had turned off the electricity. Did the police arrange for things like that after someone died? Or was it left to the next of kin or whoever ended up with the place?

I raised up on my hindquarters and put my paws on the window ledge to look inside. A red light flashed on the computer tower. I really wanted to break in and look at what could be making that fan work overtime. I pressed my nose to the pane and caught a faint whiff of cleaner. It smelled like something that would be used in an institution, like a hospital or nursing home, not in someone's home. He kept his house immaculate, which meant a guy like him might get his cleaner from an industrial source. I padded to the next window and stretched myself up to look in.

The moonlight streaming in from behind me twinkled off something shiny just under the end corner of the bed. I pushed against the glass to get a closer look—but the roar of a dually truck engine made me *yikes*. Well, not exactly a *yikes*, but as close as I could approximate in my current body. *Parker.*

I took off running into the back field, but my traitorous pit bull ran in the opposite direction. Her happy barking alerted me to the fact that she wasn't following me. *Grr.*

The engine shut off, and a truck door slammed shut.

"Lily!" Parker shouted. "If you want your dog back, you'll show yourself."

Great. No way in Samhain was I shifting back to human. Even so, I wouldn't run—I mean, I wouldn't run again—like a coward. I loped back to Doyle's house with my tail literally between my legs.

By the time I got around to the front, Smooshie, the turncoat, was already in the front seat of his truck next to Elvis, her head out the window, ears perked and tongue hanging three inches past her chin. The giant gray behemoth next to her had a stoic expression of tolerance. Poor Elvis.

I growled.

Smoosh's ears flattened guiltily, but her tongue remained visible. I shook my head. It was a good thing my pittie was adorable.

"Lily?"

I turned my head. Parker was standing about ten feet away, his eyes wide and his shoulders tightly bunched. I hissed. Why did he have to come looking for me?

"Is that really you?"

Yeah, it's really me. I hissed again.

Parker raised his hands. A move to show the animal he wasn't a threat. Gah!

He took a step toward me. My hackles rose reflexively as I took a step back.

"How much of what I'm saying can you understand? Do you know who I am? I won't hurt you," he said, his voice soft and soothing. "I'm not trying to hurt you."

Too late. I worked on breathing through my irritation. I gave Parker a pointed look then walked to the back of his truck and jumped in the bed.

"What are you doing?" Parker asked.

Isn't it obvious? I flopped down, regretting my choice when the metal riffles bit into my legs. I snarled at the smell of lawn mower gasoline coming off the push mower he had strapped down near the front of the bed and waited for him to take me home.

CHAPTER EIGHT

WHEN WE ARRIVED AT THE trailer, Parker opened my front door for me, and I growled when he tried to come inside. A few minutes later, I opened the door for him in my human form, wearing a pink fuzzy robe instead of tawny fur. Parker went back to the truck and opened the door for our companions.

"You okay?" he asked. The moonlight made his blue eyes look almost black. The steps squeaked under both dogs' weight as they preceded Parker inside.

"Why are you here, Parker?" I shoved my shaking hands into the robe pockets.

"You're so beautiful, Lils."

"That's not an answer." I crossed my arms. I didn't want to be mad at him, especially over something that wasn't his fault, but I couldn't get Naomi's smug face out of my head. My dad always said, "Werecougars have a long memory." He wasn't kidding. Mine is practically photogenic, and once an image has solidified, it's pretty much there to stay. "Is that why you drove all the way out here? To tell me how beautiful I am?"

He shook his head and gave me a small smile. "I heard you found another body."

I raised a brow. "It's not like I'm a magnet."

"I think there's a certain sheriff who might disagree."

I chuckled because I couldn't help myself. I was acting like a brat, and I knew it. I didn't usually wallow in self-pity, so I tightened my proverbial bootstraps and decided to be mature about Parker having a past social life. I dropped my hands to my sides. "Well, since you're here. You might as well come in. I might have a soda in the fridge. I have a new pack of bully sticks to keep Elvis and Smoosh busy for a bit, as well."

"Are these bully sticks made from elephant penises because I can't see anything less keeping those two busy for any amount of time."

I laughed. "I said a bit. How long are you planning on staying?"

"As long as you'll let me."

My skin shivered with pleasure. "That sounds nice."

Parker said, "Did you understand me when I found you at Doyle's?"

I'd anticipated this question. "Yes, I understood every word you were saying to me."

"Then why didn't you..." he made a wavy gesture with his hand, "...you know."

"Uhm, my clothing doesn't change with me." Duh.

"Oh." Parker's ears reddened. "I'm... I'm not." He shook his head and sat down on the couch. "I'd almost convinced myself you being what you are was all in my head."

"Seriously?" I mean, I'd let him touch my fur. It didn't get more real than in-your- face skin-shifting.

He gave me a sheepish look. "Not really. I don't know. It's a lot to take in." He paused, but I didn't leap in to fill the space. Whatever Parker wanted to say, I was going to let him. After a few seconds, he said, "Does it hurt when you become the cat?"

"Cougar," I corrected. "Or mountain lion. I guess that's the more common name in these parts."

"Okay. Cougar," he repeated. "So, does it hurt you?"

"No," I replied honestly. "Just the opposite. It's the most wonderful feeling in the world." Oh, my God. This was happening. We were finally having the conversation. My stomach grew jittery as my nerves threatened to overtake my courage, but I was determined to tell him the absolute truth, no matter what he asked.

"Where you come from, are there more of you?" He shook his head. "I mean more like you?"

I smiled. "A whole town of more like me. Not all werecougars, of course." I thought of my BFF Hazel Kinsey. "And not all Shifters either."

"What do you mean?"

Shoot. I didn't have a right to out witches as well as Shifters, but I didn't want to lie to Parker, not even by omission. "The town is half witches and half Shifters. My best friend from back home is a witch."

"A witch?" He rubbed his hand over his face. "You mean like a dance-naked-in-the-moonlight-around-a-campfire witch?"

I took out two colas from the fridge. "No. And not a ride-on-a-broomstick-wearing-a-pointy-black-hat kind of witch either, though there are a few of them that could give the myth a run for its money in the wicked department." I walked the five feet to the living room area and handed Parker one of the cans.

"What about the black cat?"

"Some witches have cat familiars. My friend Hazel has a talking squirrel."

He snorted. "That can't be true."

I crossed my heart. "Goddess strike me if I'm lying. Tizzy is a hoot. She and Hazel are the only part of home I miss."

"What made you leave?"

"I told you about my brother." Sorta. I hadn't gotten into the fact that he'd been tortured until he was unrecognizable so that his pain could power a druid spell, but I'm pretty sure I'd covered the dead part. "Our parents died eighteen years ago, so after Danny died, there wasn't much left for me in Iowa."

Parker solemnly nodded then went completely still. "Your parents died eighteen years ago? You said they died your senior year of high school."

"Oh, yeah." I worried my lower lip between my teeth then sighed. "I'm going to turn thirty-seven in August."

"That's impossible. You look younger than me."

I shrugged. "I bet up until about two months ago, you would have thought someone turning into a cougar was impossible."

"You'd be right about that." He moved over to the couch and patted the cushion next to him. "Why don't you sit a spell?"

I sat down, suddenly nervous. "Do you have any more questions?"

"A million of them," Parker said. "But right now, I'd like to hear about Donnie Doyle. Are you okay? I tried to call you, but I guess your fur suit doesn't have pockets." He grinned.

"You're right about the fur suit, but also, I broke my phone on Doyle's sidewalk." Smooshie leaned her body between my knees and against the couch.

She put her head on my thigh. I put my hand on her head automatically. "This one yanked me forward when I tried to call Nadine about the smell."

"The smell?"

"Death, decay, etcetera." I wrinkled my nose. "I could smell it before I'd even made it to the front door."

"Yuck."

"You said it."

"So, you decided to go in and check on things yourself."

"Are you lecturing me?"

"Not at all." He held up his hands. "Just getting the whole picture."

"Doyle's phone started ringing."

"And you went inside to answer it?"

I narrowed my gaze at Parker. "You are starting to sound a lot like Sheriff Avery."

"Ouch. You wound me." He smiled then shook his head. "Can't believe we got another body in Moonrise. At least the guy has a good excuse for abandoning his dog. And, at least this death is accidental."

I raised a brow at him.

"Not accidental?"

"I have my doubts."

"Is that why you went over there tonight?"

I shook my head. "I went over there to run away from you."

His brows arched with surprise. "Why would you want to do a thing like that?"

Because I am petty and jealous. "I wasn't in the mood to talk." Not a lie.

"I can imagine. This is all so fantastic. It's hard to wrap my brain around it."

"It's not that."

"Then what?"

"Did you sleep with Naomi?"

His brows rose higher.

Okay, he didn't deny it. My nerves got the better of me, and I blurted, "Because I ran into her tonight and she basically said you had."

"And you believed her?"

"No. Not really. But she didn't act like she was lying." I met his gaze. I wanted to tell him about the witch magic that made it easy for me to tell if someone was lying, but I figured that was a conversation for another day. "Did you sleep with her on that date?"

"No." He gave me a crooked smile and shook his head. "I did not sleep, have sex, or do anything with

Naomi the night we went out." His eyes softened at the corners. "Do you believe me?"

My lie-o-meter stayed dormant, but it always did with Parker. He was either super honest, or it didn't work with him. I believe both might be the case. "I do." The tightness in my chest eased. "But she's very convincing."

"I won't lie to you, Lily. Ever."

"Thanks." I felt a pinch of guilt for all my secrets. I took a long drink of my cola to calm my nerves and belched loudly. "Wow. Sorry."

Parker laughed. "I think you registered a seven on the Richter scale with that one."

I shook my head. "I hope I didn't trigger the New Madrid fault. I'd hate to be responsible for Moonrise falling into the earth."

I'll admit, I enjoyed the relaxed banter with Parker, but it also made me anxious. His calm demeanor made me feel unbalanced. I'd become accustomed to Broody Parker, Distant Parker, and Silent Parker, so Easy Going Parker kind of freaked me out. I braced myself for the inevitable other shoe drop.

He put his hand on mine. "Are you planning to put yourself in danger again?"

I tingled under his touch. "That's never my plan."

He leaned closer to me, his face inches from mine. My breath caught in my throat when he said, "I'd really like to kiss you, Lily Mason."

If I'd been standing my knees would have buckled. I closed the distance between us, the heat of his lips warming me to the core. He deepened the kiss, and I eased into him, my shoulder pressing against his chest. His five o'clock shadow scratched my chin and cheeks, which only made me want him more. His arms slid around my waist. I turned, not wanting to break that contact with his body, not wanting the kiss to end. It wasn't enough. I wanted more, my cougar rose to the surface.

Then I tasted blood. I drew my face back from Parker's chasing lips. "I…I think I might have bit you."

"I don't care," he said breathlessly. His eyelids drooped heavy lidded with desire. My robe slid off my shoulder, and Parker caressed my bare skin with his fingers. He gave me a sexy half-smile. "I really don't."

I pressed my swollen lips together and took a deep breath in through my nose to calm the tingles I felt all over. It had been a very long time since I'd kissed anyone except for those two times with Parker, and never in my life had I been kissed the way he'd just kissed me. "Okay." I smiled shyly and lifted my chin for another.

The phone rang. No, not my phone. Parker's. I was beginning to feel like I had a curse on me where the man was concerned.

"It'll go to voice mail," he said.

"But what if it's the shelter? Or your dad?" Ugh. I hated myself more than I can say right then.

Parker sighed, loudly. He reached into his back pocket and pulled out his cell. It was an old-fashioned flip phone, the kind built for construction workers, great reception, durable as hell, and no bells and whistles. What was it with the men of Moonrise? He and my uncle both needed to join the twenty-first century—said the girl whose phone broke the minute it hit the sidewalk.

He opened it, looked at the caller ID then back to me. "It's the shelter. Jerry's there this evening." He hit the green button. "Parker here," he said.

Jerry asked, "Where are you at?" Panic filled the volunteer's voice.

Parker raised his brow at me. "I'm out. What's wrong?"

I didn't know Jerry as well as I did the other volunteers, as we rarely worked the same shifts, but as a fireman, I would think he was hard to rattle. I leaned forward, anticipating the worst.

"Someone tried to break into the building while I was outside with Star. The key safe is busted off the door. They couldn't get it open, but the ding on the metal makes me think they tried. I heard the front door groaning when I came back inside, and it took me several minutes to get it open. There are pry marks near the deadbolt. Whoever done it, bent the frame, which is why it stuck."

"Did you see who?" Parker stood up now and adjusted his jeans.

"No. They were gone by the time I could look. But I was cussing up a storm, so they had a warning I was coming."

"Did you call the police?"

"I wasn't sure you'd want me to, not after last fall."

Jerry was referring to the time a dead woman was found in Parker's backyard. Parker had been a suspect in the death. Things had taken an ugly turn when he was arrested and jailed for a couple of days. That was my first encounter with a dead body. I wish it had been my last.

"I'll head over now. Let me look around before we bring the sheriff's department into the mix."

"You got it, Parker. I'll see you in…"

"Fifteen-twenty minutes." Parker hung up the phone and look down at me. "You coming?"

"Sure." I might be able to catch a scent or clue that someone else would miss. "Give me a minute to get some clothes on."

Parker sighed again. Loudly.

I smiled like the cat who ate the canary.

CHAPTER NINE

OTHER THAN DAMAGE to the key safe and the door, there didn't seem to be anything else amiss. Jerry was in a high state of agitation. He was a tall, thickly built man with dirty blond hair and a short beard.

His eyes crinkled at the corners, and his brow furrowed with deep lines. "I swear, if I find out who tried to break in…"

Parker put his hand on Jerry's shoulder. "I'm just glad you were here to prevent the person from entering. No telling what would have happened." Elvis hugged Parker's legs. He could sense the tension coming from all of us.

I shook my head. The break-in made absolutely no sense. "Why would someone want to break into the shelter? We have less than two hundred in petty cash."

"People want pit bulls for all sorts of reasons, and some of the reasons are pretty bad," Parker said.

"Most likely, they were looking for dogs to fight or to breed."

I thought about Star. Her condition when she'd arrived had been nothing short of awful. She'd been overbred by an illegal puppy mill.

Smooshie's tail hit my leg, and I reached down to stroke her fur. She had scars on her face from her life before rescue. Had she been used as a fighting dog? The idea made me sick to my stomach. "Don't those idiots know we spay and neuter every dog that comes to us?" I clenched my fists, my claws cutting into my palms. "There's a special place in the afterlife for people who use these dogs for anything more than loving companions." I'd seen a lot of evil in my life, but people who treated animals cruelly were true devils.

"The key safe did its job. It looks like the burglar took a sledgehammer to it. Knocked it off the wall but didn't do any real damage to the actual contraption," Jerry said. His bushy brows furrowed. "I sure wish I could've gotten my hands on the guy."

"What makes you think it was a man?" I asked.

Jerry pursed his lips and looked up for a moment. After a few seconds, he said, "I don't know. I guess it could have been a woman, but I think it takes some strength to wield a sledgehammer high enough and hard enough to knock the key safe down."

"They probably wore gloves, but even if they didn't, the police won't do much. Not on a thwarted breaking-and-entering case. Nothing was taken, and there isn't any more damage, so…" Parker shrugged. I knew he didn't want to have to deal with Sheriff Avery again. His short stint in the county jail had been traumatizing, especially with his PTSD. It made him wary of involving the sheriff's department in his business.

"We should probably look into getting some security cameras," I told him.

"That's a good idea," Parker said.

Jerry nodded his head, his face serious in thought. "Those security systems can get pricey."

Parker half-smiled. "I might know a guy."

His wistful expression made me wonder if the guy was an ex-Ranger buddy. Elvis nudged Parker's hand, and he absently patted his companion, reminding me that my own companion would expect me home soon.

"I can call Buzz to run me back to my place," I said. "You have your hands full fixing the door."

Jerry piped up. "I'll take you. I live out past your place."

The revelation surprised me. Jerry and I had only talked in passing, and the conversation usually involved casual greetings and dog talk. I gave Jerry an appraising look then smiled. "I appreciate the offer. Thanks."

Parker put his hand on my arm and his voice slightly deepened. "I hope we can continue where we left off. Soon."

My smile broadened into a grin. Aware Jerry watched us with curiosity, I said, "We have that dinner on Sunday. We can talk more then."

Jerry walked me out to his truck, and we headed toward our respective homes. Jerry's conversational skills ran to casual caveman. He did a lot of grunting either yes or no or short answer to most of my small-talk questions. How long had he been married? Twelve years. Did he have kids? Yes. Did he grow up in Moonrise? No. He wasn't cold. Just the opposite really. His responses were friendly, even if brief. When we passed Doyle's road, Jerry said, "I hear you found the kid."

Considering it was the most words he'd strung together since our journey home started, his comment took me by surprise. "Yes," I said, taking a page from his book.

The side of his mouth quirked up. "I've heard some wild stories."

"From who?"

"My wife." Jerry blinked as if his answer astonished him.

I hadn't meant to use my witch magic to compel the truth. I'd acted automatically. Instinct mixed with curiosity. "What has she told you?" I pushed my desire for answers toward him.

"She said he got around with a lot of the local women. He wasn't too discriminating either. Young, older, single, or married. He had a taste for it all." He blinked again.

I ignored the creeping guilt. My power didn't have much teeth if the person I used it on didn't want to talk. Which meant, on some level, Jerry had wanted to spill this information to someone. "Did she mention anyone in particular?"

"Rachel." His expression had grown bland.

I was pushing too hard, but I needed a little more information. Donnie had called the drunk woman from the bar Rachel. I needed a last name, but before I could ask, Jerry said, "That's your drive up ahead, right?"

"Yes, that's it." I smiled. "Thanks for the lift, Jerry. I appreciate it. Oh, how is your wife doing?" I asked to ease his tension. My magic could push some people to the point of shutting down. "Parker told me she'd been in the hospital recently."

"Yes," he said. "Pneumonia. It came on all of a sudden, but she's better now." He squinted at me then focused on his fingers gripping the steering wheel. "I don't usually talk out of turn, Lily. I hope you won't hold it against me."

Guilt turned inside me. "It's been an exciting night. Adrenaline can make anyone chatty."

I got out and waved goodbye. Donnie hadn't been choosy about his bedmates. No surprise there. Had he been killed by a jealous lover? A jealous husband? Boyfriend?

Smooshie's whining inside the trailer distracted me from the questions tumbling through my thoughts. "I'm coming, girl," I said, smiling as she replied with happy yips.

****

I didn't sleep a wink during the night. Between thoughts of a dead Donnie Doyle, Parker's visit to my trailer, the break-in at the kennel, and Donnie's sordid love life, I couldn't turn my brain off. I was glad I had the day to myself. I wasn't sure how to be around Parker at the rescue center now that we were taking real steps to date. I mean, would we keep it on the down low or was he okay with the other staff and volunteers knowing?

I got up at six a.m., showered and dressed, let Smooshie out to potty, before getting us both on the road to town. Nadine, who had the day off, had offered to babysit the baby while I took my GED exam. Since the test was so long, asking Nadine to watch my girl all day was a big ask. It might have been easier to drop her off with Parker, but I still wasn't ready to tell him that I'd dropped out of high school my senior year and never graduated. Our conversation the night before, when I'd told him about my parents and Danny, had given me the perfect segue. Still, I'd left it out. I'd tell him on Sunday over spaghetti.

I smiled to myself. Smooshie's tail whacked me on the thigh. I glanced her way. "Quit reading my mind." She licked my hand when I scratched her cheek. "You ready to terrorize, Auntie Nadine?"

Smooshie barked a happy bark, her whole body vibrating with visible excitement. Auntie Nadine liked to sneak her treats. I pulled into Buzz and Nadine's driveway at six forty-five in the morning and parked behind Nadine's red VW Bug.

"Hey, Smoosh!" Nadine said from the open front door.

I reached over and opened the passenger door. Smooshie jumped out and ran to Nadine for cuddles. I loved how my friend loved my pittie.

"What am I?" I said when I got out of the truck. "Chopped beef?"

"Hey, Lils," Nadine smiled. "When do you have to be out at the college?"

"At eight, but I have to stop by Walmart first to replace my cell phone."

"That doesn't give you much time. You better just get down to the college and forget about Walmart."

"I really need a phone."

"Well, just don't dawdle. You don't want to have to pay to take the test again."

I gave her a hug. "I can't believe I'm actually doing this. Is this crazy? What if I can't pass the test?"

"You're one of the smartest people I know. You'll pass that test with flying colors."

"I'm glad you have faith." I'd taken a few practice exams and struggled. It seemed while I held a lot of knowledge in my brain, but when I tried to use it during the quizzes, my mind would go blank.

I said my goodbyes to Nadine and Smoosh, who managed to wet-willy me with her tongue when I hugged her neck, and then headed out to Walmart.

The store was unsurprisingly busy for a Saturday. "Hey, there," Wanda, according to her name badge, the Walmart greeter said as I walked through the automatic sliding doors.

"Hey," I said back, but she'd already moved on to the people coming in behind me. I bee-lined down the aisle between women's clothes and the grocery side then took a sharp right to electronics.

The phone section had fifteen options. I gravitated toward the cheapest smartphone. I didn't need a ton of bells and whistles. Besides, I couldn't really afford to drop seven hundred dollars on a phone, not when I needed every last extra cent for reconstruction on my fixer-upper home.

"Can I help you?" A woman with straight brown hair and a blue vest stood on the employee side of the phone display. It took me a second, but I recognized her as the woman from the bar who'd fought with Donnie. Her badge said, *Rachel.*

"Hi, yes," I said, quickly recovering from my initial surprise. "I'm looking for a phone."

"Then you're in the right place." She gave me a tight smile. Her red-rimmed brown eyes gave me a cursory glance before she turned them down toward the counter. "Any phone in particular, or do you want me to help you pick one?"

Even though I'd already made my choice, I said, "Sure. What do you recommend?"

"It depends on what you want." Rachel shrugged then sniffled. "I'm sorry. I'm crap help today." She met my gaze. "Do you want an Android or iOS?"

"I'm not sure," I lied. I pushed my ancestor's mojo into my next words, searching for the truth. "Are you okay?"

Rachel grabbed a tissue and blew her nose. "Not really. I lost someone recently."

"I'm so sorry." I touched the back of her hand. Most likely, she was talking about Doyle, but just in case her mom died, too, I asked, "Was it a relative?"

"No." A tear rolled down her cheek. "He...he was my..." She stopped short of a definition. "I loved him."

True. But you can love someone and still kill them, especially if spurned. What I'd seen go down between them at the bar had spurned written all over it. "I don't mean to pry..." although, I really did, "...but how did he die?"

"I don't know," she said despondently. "I've picked up my phone to call the police so many times, but I can't. My husband..." She held her hands out in a gesture of hopelessness.

Damn. Rachel was married.

"Did your husband know?"

"No," she said before her gaze turned sharp. "I don't want to talk about this anymore."

I'd been pushing too hard, and her subconscious pushed back. "Of course." I looked down at the phone I'd already chosen. "I'll take this one. It's in my budget." Barely. Even as one of the cheaper models, it would take a decent bite out of my checking account.

I told her my carrier and signed a phone agreement, giving Rachel a moment. I could sense she was holding something back. My ability encouraged the truth from people, but there are some secrets that even magic can't reveal. "I found his body."

Rachel dropped the phone she'd retrieved and stared at me with something akin to pain and horror. "Who? Whose body?"

"Donald Doyle." She winced as if slapped, and I cringed at my own cruelty, but finding the truth wasn't always kind. "He's the friend you lost, right?"

She wrung her hands together, and her eyes narrowed at me. "How did you…"

"I saw you with him at Dally's last Tuesday night." When she gave me another startled look, I added, "You were fighting with him. It was hard not to notice."

Rachel shook her head. "I…he…" She took a deep breath and closed her eyes for a moment to calm herself. When she was composed, she said, "We'd had a simple misunderstanding."

My skin buzzed, the hair standing on end. Her claim of a "simple misunderstanding" was a lie. I put compassion into my words because my aim wasn't to hurt her more. "You were very upset. Look, my best friend is a deputy at the sheriff's department. If you're uncomfortable coming forward with information because of your husband, I could help you."

"How did he die?" she asked suddenly, as if my earlier words about finding the body had just sunk in. "I need to know."

As a Shifter, touch was a comfort. I didn't know Rachel, but I knew the pain of loss. I placed my hand on her forearm. "I don't know how he died. There is some evidence it was an accident." There was also some indication he was killed, and the scene staged, but I kept that to myself. If the sheriff caught wind I was spreading rumors about an open case, he'd probably find a way to lock me up for obstruction of justice. "When was the last time you saw him?"

She blushed. "Not since that night at the bar."

It was a partial truth. I gave her forearm a squeeze. I kept my voice gentle as if she were a fragile eggshell. "You know something, don't you?"

Rachel tensed then opened the new phone box. "Do you have your phone with you? I'll switch over your SIM card."

I was close to the secret she didn't want anyone to know. Secrets ate at most people. The fact that she was holding on so tightly meant it was horrendous, or at least, Rachel thought so. "There's a memory card in there, too." I pulled my broken phone from my purse and handed it to her. "I have pictures of my baby I don't want to lose."

She smiled, the creases around her eyes lessened. "You have a kid? How old?"

"She's about three now." I laughed. "And covered in fur. My baby is my dog."

"Oh," Rachel smiled. "I'm a cat person, myself."

"I like cats too." After all, I was a werecougar.

Rachel nodded. She held up the new phone. "I can move your memory card over too."

"Thanks. You really know your stuff." I watched her practiced hand open the back of one phone and move the small parts over to the other. "You were telling me about Donnie."

She raised her brow, snapped the back onto the new phone, and smirked. "Was I?" She handed me the phone. The screen was lit. "It will only take me a minute to activate it."

I held up my hand. "All right. I get it." While she was typing responses into her computer screen, I picked up a pen from the counter and pulled a scrap of paper from my purse. I scribbled my name and number. "Now that I have a phone again, you can call me if you want to talk."

CHAPTER TEN

THE KNOT IN THE PIT of my stomach doubled as I walked into the testing center. The directions on my confirmation email had said to not bring in anything but two pencils and a calculator. I didn't have the money for one of those fancy, advanced scientific-math ones, but I'd managed to get a cheaper version from the internet. How schools expected people to spend more than a day's wages on a piece of technology that would only get used for a brief period of time was beyond me. It seemed like something schools should have available to check out for people with modest means.

Calming my jitters would have been easier if I was more confident. I knew the material, I told myself. I could do this.

Mr. Kirkshaw, the financial aid manager, stood by the door to the testing room. I recognized him because he was the person I'd paid my ninety-five dollars in order to take the test.

He tapped a computer pen against his tablet. "I need to see your confirmation paperwork." He barely made eye contact with me. His scent was a mixture of bathroom deodorizer and acidic body odor. His halitosis made me wince. Mr. Kirkshaw needed to take better care of his health. There was a slight yellow tinge to his skin and sclera, and he had broken blood vessels over his nose. The bulge around his middle, on such a thin man, was prominent. Combine the odor, the color, and his belly bloat, and you had a man who probably drank too much on a regular basis. Whatever the cause of his ailment, his liver was certainly damaged.

He looked over my paperwork. "Go on in and find a seat. The testing will begin in a few minutes."

"Thank you, sir." Kirkshaw was probably close to my age in actual years, but I'd been taught to respect authority.

"Good luck," he said before turning his attention to the lanky guy behind me. "Confirmation," I heard him say as I went inside and sat at one of the middle desks. Not too close to draw attention to myself, but not so far back I missed any information.

In the back right, I noticed a familiar face, one I certainly hadn't expected. Lacy Evans.

I knew three things about Lacy. She worked as a legal secretary, was a bit of a party girl, and she was a crap mom. Thank heavens Freda, her mother, played a huge role in the boy's life. Once, Lacy had wrecked her car running to the store while her baby was home alone. Did I mention she'd almost hit me as well?

I wondered if I could get a refund on the test if I snuck out. Lacy was also a gossip and a mean girl. I could see her using my lack of education as a way to poke at me. Of course, she had dropped out of school as well, obviously. Maybe we could call for a Reagan throw-back Mutually Assured Destruction if either of us told anyone.

Frankly, I was surprised she was a dropout. How had she managed to get her job with Jock Simmons? I hated to hazard a guess because that sleazeball probably had ulterior motives. Maybe she was really trying to change her life. Kind of like me. Hell, I admired Lacy for trying to get her GED. As a matter of fact, I admired everyone in the room. It was no easy task taking steps backward to move forward, but that's what all of us were doing here this morning.

I decided to pretend like I didn't see Lacy. If she wanted to approach me, so be it, but otherwise, I would ignore her.

I took a deep breath to steady my nerves, placed my calculator and pencils on the desk in front of me and waited for the instructor to tell us what came next. At a few minutes to eight, Ms. Lovell walked inside.

"Good morning," she said brightly. "Are we all ready to embrace the future today?"

That seemed an ambitious task, but I nodded my head, along with most of the students.

"Excellent." I need you to store jackets, phones, and purses or backpacks under your chair. You can retrieve them when the test has concluded."

Two people put light jackets under their chairs. It had been warm out today, so the jackets made no sense. But my body heat ran higher than a human's, so what did I know.

We'd been given short breaks in between the three sections we were tested on, but come three o'clock in the afternoon, I'd had my fill of test-taking to last me a lifetime. Or until I had to take the damn test again. I stood up from my seat and walked out of the room feeling dejected. There were too many questions that I had gone back to multiple times to change the answer, and I was certain I'd blown it.

I turned my phone on as I made my way out onto the campus toward the parking lot. I had a missed call from Parker. I called him back before I reached my truck.

"Hey, Parker. Did anything come up missing from the break-in?"

"No," he said. "I got the locks changed out. Do you think you can come by the shelter this evening? Jerry got called in to take an extra shift at the fire department, and I'm having trouble getting anyone else in on short notice. I would do it myself, but I promised Dad I would meet him for dinner. He has something he wants to talk to me about."

"Sure. I'm happy to help." Besides, it wasn't like I had a hot date, considering my hot date was taking his dad to dinner.

"Have you heard any more about Doyle?"

"Nothing."

After a brief pause, Parker asked, "I'm sorry you're the one who found him, Lily. It had to be awful for you."

"Thanks." His words were like a hug, and one that I sorely needed. "What time do you want me there?"

"Five-thirty or so."

"You got it."

****

By the time I picked Smooshie up from Nadine's, I had about two hours until I had to be at the shelter. Just enough time for a short detour. I headed out of town and drove out toward my house and turned down Doyle's road, knowing it was a bad idea but doing it anyway. I'd spotted something shiny through his window the night before, but Parker's arrival had stopped me from investigating further. Well, that and the fact that I was on all fours and covered in fur. I know the police had done a cursory search of Donnie's place, but they might have overlooked something that I could detect with my enhanced senses.

In the bright morning light, Donnie's house once again looked like a place where a retired couple might live. The flowers were well tended, the grass slightly overgrown but neat, and the ranch-style home. I pulled into the driveway. Smooshie began to whine, her tail swishing with expectant and excited energy. I sometimes think that the dog enjoyed it when I put our collective noses where they didn't belong.

I opened the driver door, and Smoosh was on my lap and jumping out before I could get a foot down. She ran to the door of the house. Maybe she was hoping for another dead body.

I reached into my purse for the training clicker and gave it a push. Smoosh barked once at the closed front door then ran back to me. "You have to stay with me, girl. No snooping around on your own."

She cocked her head sideways, her right ear twitching, as a big smile cut her broad jaw. I clipped her leash onto her collar, thankful Doyle lived out far enough to avoid nosy neighbors, you know, like me. The front door was locked. No surprise there. I searched around the porch, under the welcome mat, and in the pot of a plant near the door. No extra key. Maybe Doyle hadn't kept one.

A hard tug from Smooshie nearly yanked me off my feet. She began digging in the flowerbed. "No," I chided. "Not here." I didn't mind her digging, but I wasn't trying to advertise our attempted B&E.

I stepped down into the dirt, squatting to fill in the area Smooshie's big paws had scooped, when I noticed a smooth rock like what you'd find in a creek bed, near the brick skirt. On instinct, I turned it over, a surge of triumph rising inside me when I saw a key holder on the bottom.

Smooshie leaped onto the porch like a bull in a rodeo. I retrieved the key and tried it in the door. "Hah!" I did a minor celebratory shimmy and scratched her ear. "Good girl, Smoosh!"

Inside, the smell of death was less pungent, but it still made me queasy. I locked the door behind me just in case anyone stopped by while I was here. It was bad enough finding the body, I didn't need the police catching me snooping around.

I stepped around the area where I'd found Donnie's body and made my way to the sink. The cup I'd noticed was still there. I picked it up and sniffed it. There was a faint citrus odor, but more like a detergent than actual fruit. Nadine had been right about the cup in the sink. It was squeaky clean. The entire kitchen shined. Living on a gravel road meant constant dust, and I didn't see hardly any in Doyle's kitchen. I opened drawers under the counters. Even his utility drawer was neat and organized, and I didn't see any personal items like photos or mementos. The Donnie I'd met at the bar had seemed warm and friendly, approachable, but his house was sanitized.

And yet, a clean glass sat in the sink. It seemed out of the ordinary for someone who labeled their dry goods and put them in alphabetical order. If he had OCD, he hid it well as a server in a crowded bar. I thought of the noise, the spills, the sticky floors, and empty beer bottles. Nope. No way was that kid the OCD type. This cleanliness felt unnatural.

I tugged Smooshie back from the oil spot on the ground, the one Donnie had supposedly slipped in, and knelt down next to it. "What do you make of this?" I asked the dog without an expectation of an answer. I touched the middle surface and rubbed it between my fingertips. It was thicker than regular vegetable oil. I smelled it. It had a slightly sweet and nutty aroma. Hazelnut? Unusual, but nice.

After I finished in the kitchen, I made my way to the office since it was the first room when I entered the hall. I could still hear the mechanical sound of the computer fan blade as it whirred around. I sat down in the desk chair and moved the mouse around the pad to wake up the monitor. The police would have already fingerprinted this place, and the fact that I found the body and used the phone in here to call nine-one-one made wearing gloves moot.

Wow. I think I'd gone past nosy and right into none-of-my-business. I was thinking forensically—I wondered if Hazel would be proud or horrified of me.

Smooshie crawled under the desk and shoved her big head between my knees so she could rest her chin on my thigh. Chances were Doyle's computer was password protected, which meant I'd find a fat lot of nothing.

As I'd suspected, a bar came up, and it asked for a passcode. I had a basic knowledge of computers and the internet, enough to look up stuff on a search engine and send emails. Cracking passwords was not in my wheelhouse. I opened the drawers starting from top to bottom. All but the third out of four drawers slid out with ease. The third had a lock with tool marks and scratches at the opening. Picking locks wasn't in my wheelhouse, either, but it looked like someone had tried to jimmy the drawer before. I found a paper clip in the middle drawer and tried wiggling it around the damaged keyhole to see if that got me anywhere. I even extended one of my claws and tried to open the drawer that way.

Nope. Nada. Not at all. I might possibly be the world's worse private eye or criminal. Sure, I knew how to break in, but the "entering" part was not my forte. Still, I was no quitter. I began looking through the drawers more thoroughly, looking under the organizers, paperwork, and books. The open drawers where getting me nowhere. I had to get in that locked one. I thought about the way Donnie had hidden the house key. I felt under all the drawers, and on the last one, I found a magnetic key holder.

I took the key out and slid it into the lock. It took a little jiggling, probably because of the damage, but it finally turned. Inside the drawer, I found four new, unopened 500GB USB drives and a receipt from Walmart for them. Why would he have those locked up? They hadn't even been used.

I placed the drives on the desk and noticed a small dark object at the back of the drawer. It was a plastic cap, and it looked similar to the tops of the unopened drives. Had the person who'd damaged the lock actually manage to get inside and take whatever used drives had been in here? That didn't make sense—if they'd managed to break open the drawer, then it wouldn't still be locked. Maybe they'd found the key like I had. And tried to put things back. You know, like I was.

I put everything back the way I'd found it and locked the drawer up and replaced the key, then went to the bedroom next. I went through each drawer as I had the desk. Nothing but clothing, which had been neatly folded and organized by size and color.

I got down on all fours and reached my hand under the bed where I'd seen the sparkle the night before. It was a large hoop earring, with an unmistakable crisscrossing pattern. My stomach dropped.

It was Reggie's.

Maybe she'd lost it when she'd come to examine the body.

I shook my head. No. When she'd arrived at the crime scene, she hadn't been wearing the hoops. For that matter, I hadn't seen her wearing those earrings since our girls' night out last Tuesday. Crap.

I pocketed the hoop and searched the rest of the room for more evidence that might implicate that my friend had a more-than-professional relationship with the deceased.

*****

I locked up Donnie's house, put the key back under the rock, then drove straight to Reggie's home. Smooshie laid her head across my lap, curiously quiet. I knew she felt the thread of tension running through me. Reggie's house was a three-bedroom, three-car-garage mini-mansion. At least, it was a mansion compared to the shack I'd bought. Smooshie and I got out and strode to the front door. I rang the doorbell. Then again. And again. And a couple more times after that.

I heard Reggie holler, "Just a damn minute."

I glanced down a Smoosh. "Maybe the five rings were overkill."

The dog's tongue lolled out the side of her mouth, and she panted hard, which I interpreted to mean, *probably*.

The front door flung open. Reggie's hair was trussed up in a towel, she wore a fuzzy purple robe and matching slippers, and she held a pint of melting Chunky Monkey ice scream in one of her hands. Her narrowed brow softened when she saw it was me. "Lily." She blinked. The bags under her eyes were dark, as if she hadn't slept in two days. "Were we supposed to get together today?"

I held out her earring.

Her face reddened, and she teared up.

"I think you better invite us in," I said.

Reggie nodded. "Come on in."

CHAPTER ELEVEN

REGGIE FUMBLED THE HOOP between her fingers for a few silent moments. I gave her time to gather her thoughts and emotions.

Suddenly, as if it were a live coal, she thrust the hoop at me. "You should give this to the police. It's material evidence from a crime scene." Her cheeks splotched with color. "Why didn't you turn this in?"

"First," I told her. "Who you have relations with is no one's business. Second, I don't believe for a second that you had anything to do with Doyle's death. And third, I acquired this item in a way that Sheriff Avery would frown upon. Finally, if you did have anything to do with his death, I'm sure you had a perfectly good reason, and friends help friends hide incriminating evidence." I placed the hoop back into her palm and closed her fingers around it.

Reggie's lips parted, closed, then parted again. Abruptly, she began to laugh and cry at the same time. Relief and mild hysteria, if I had to guess. "I didn't kill him. I barely remembered his house until I walked in the other night." She rubbed her face. "One stupid night with a man young enough to be my—"

"Younger brother," I filled in. She'd beat herself up enough already. "He was a nice-looking man." I emphasized "man" because, while Donnie was young, he was only a year younger than Parker, and I'd never thought of Parker as a boy. "He was charming and flirting, and you'd had a bad day dealing with your ex-husband. If anyone deserves a little fun, it's you. So, stop being so hard on yourself."

"I haven't even done the autopsy, yet. I couldn't bring myself to cut into someone I'd had sex with."

"I can imagine. Maybe you can ask someone else to step in."

"With what excuse?" She shook her head. "I have to tell the sheriff about my involvement."

I knew Sheriff Avery well enough to know that nothing good would come of Reggie's confession. "Look. You are a darn good doctor. People count on you in this town. You go spilling your guts about your one-night stand with Donnie and it will be all over town, and after the last homicidal coroner, I don't think the office can take any more scandal."

"It might be too late for that already." Her elegant features were marred by the worry lines etched across her brow. Smooshie, who'd been a very good girl since we'd arrived, crawled up on the couch next to Reggie and put her head on Reggie's lap. I could see the tension ease from her shoulders as she stroked the pit bull with her manicured fingers. "I think someone might already know."

I leaned forward. "What do you mean?"

Reggie sighed. "I got a letter about four days ago. I wasn't sure what it meant, but now I think it's pretty clear."

"What did it say?"

"I know what you did and soon everyone will."

I raised a brow. "Do you still have this note?"

She shook her head. "No. I thought it was a prank. I couldn't imagine what anyone might know about me that my ex's lawyers hadn't already uncovered. Those jerks tore into my deepest closets and excavated any skeletons I might have had. I didn't even think about my night with Donnie. I mean, it was just a fun time, that's all. It didn't mean anything." She covered her eyes for a moment with the hand that wasn't stroking Smooshie's neck. "Gah. I hate saying it didn't mean anything, but it didn't. That poor guy is dead, and our brief interaction was a blip on my radar. Nothing more than an ego boost for a middle-aged woman who needed to be wanted."

"I can't stand how your ex-husband has torn you down and made you feel like you're somehow less than. You are sexy as hell, Reggie Crawford, for a woman of any age. Plenty of men would want you. You've just got to open your eyes."

A slight smile tugged at the corners of her lips. "I hope you're right."

"Wait a minute." I sat up straight. "What are you not telling me?"

"Oh," she said nervously. "I didn't want to say anything in case nothing came of it."

I shook my head. "Well, now you have to tell me."

"Let's just say that my encounter with Donnie gave me the courage to ask out the man I'm really interested in. As a matter of record, I was on a date with him the night you found the body."

"And?"

"And it had been going really well up until the phone call from the police department. Hah!"

I remembered how nice she'd looked when she'd arrived on the scene. And her scent, there were parts that didn't quite fit her perfume but had smelled familiar.

I remembered a certain dog sitter that night had been showered up and perfumed with cologne. "Greer?"

A flash of pink rose in Reggie's cheeks. "Yes." She smiled then frowned. "If this gets out about Donnie, I don't think Greer will give me a second look. What's he going to think of me when he finds out about all this?"

Greer's wife had died of breast cancer a little over ten years ago. Parker told me once that he didn't think his dad would ever move past losing the love of his life. Had Greer been a Shifter, I might have agreed, but humans, like witches, could fall in love more than once, and a surge of happiness for him and Reggie swept over me. "That's so great. You are both two of the best people I know. And Greer is not some jerk who is going to punish you for having a life before him."

"But ten days before him? That's pretty recent history."

I didn't believe Greer would think less of Reggie for her one-night stand. "He's not the judgy kind. How did I not see this happening?" Greer was a mechanic and Reggie a doctor. Talk about opposites attracting.

"I don't know." She grew wistful. "He was changing the oil on my car one day, and I'd made a comment about not knowing a spark plug from an exhaust pipe, and Greer said that in a way we were both mechanics. We just fixed different kinds of vehicles." She laughed. "Then he wiped his cheek and smudged grease across his face. All kinds of blue-collar fantasies played in my mind. After that, I kept finding reasons to take my car to his shop. I would stay and chat with him while he did whatever needed to be done. It wasn't until this week though that I got up the nerve to ask him out on a date."

"So ballsy," I teased.

"Seriously," Reggie said. "My knees were knocking, but I'd began to think we'd both be in a nursing home long before he got around to asking me first."

Knowing Greer, she was probably right. "I don't think Donnie's death is an accident. You need to do the autopsy."

"It's a conflict of interest, Lily."

"Did you kill him?"

"No."

"Then there's no conflict."

Reggie chuckled, but not as if she were really amused. "It doesn't work like that. If it comes out that I slept with the victim, my entire medical report will lose its validation. It could cause a mistrial if the police catch the real killer. I can't do that, not even to protect myself from the humiliation of town gossip and suspicion."

"Fine," I grumbled. "Be a grown-up." In my heart, I knew Reggie was right. It was a testament to her character. A testament I hoped Greer took into consideration when the truth came out, because I really thought the two of them together were pretty damned perfect.

"You're right about one thing, though. The autopsy needs to happen soon. I'll call Dr. Azan, the M.E. in Cape Girardeau, and see if he'll come down. I did my forensic pathology fellowship with him. I trust him."

I looked at the display on my new phone. It was five after five. "Shoot. I told Parker I'd meet him by five-thirty."

"You better get going then." Reggie forced a smile as she stood up. Smooshie jumped down to the floor and waited expectantly for whatever would happen next. Reggie gave me a quick hug. "Don't keep that man waiting. He's one of the good ones."

"And so is his dad," I replied. "Greer isn't going to think any less of you."

"I hope you're right."

I hoped I was right too.

****

I gave a little sigh as I pulled into Parker's driveway. All the way over I couldn't stop thinking about Reggie and the vulnerable position she was in.

Smooshie began to whine when I didn't immediately turn the truck off. It was a warm spring day. Parker stepped out his front door wearing jeans and a muscle-hugging blue T-shirt. My foot slipped onto the gas pedal, at least that's the story I'm sticking with, and the engine revved loudly.

Smooshie barked at me as I jerked my foot back. Thank the Goddess I'd put the truck in park, or I'd have crashed right through Parker's garage door. Quickly, I turned off the engine and got out. Smooshie followed after me.

"Hey, Parker." My cheeks warmed under his curious gaze. "Sorry about that."

"What's wrong with Old Martha?"

I smiled at his use of the truck's nickname. "Sticky pedal," I fibbed. "I'll have your dad look at it sometime."

"That's a good idea." He smiled. "You look nice today."

"As opposed to other days?" I teased.

Parker stammered, "I didn't mean…"

"I'm just messing with you." Smooshie hunched her back and pooped on Parker's front lawn. A blue sedan slowed down as it passed Parker's home. Smooshie dropped several turds, undeterred by the audience. The car sped up a few feet past the driveway and turned left at the four-way at the end of the street.

Parker crossed his arms, his biceps bulging. "I guess that wasn't the Nelsons."

Smooshie, now several ounces lighter, happily zipped back in forth in a speedy race of joy. I stared at the steaming pile she'd left behind. "I don't have a doodoo bag on me. Do you?"

"Ah, leave it." Parker waved his hand in Smoosh's direction. "I'll get it later with the mower."

"She really has no manners." I didn't help that I pretty much let her poop wherever she wanted as long as it wasn't indoors.

From next door at the shelter, Addy and CeCe burst through the front door, Addy holding the pup under his right arm and carrying something floppy with his left hand. "Parker!" he shouted when he saw us. "Lily!"

Both kids looked out of breath and a little freaked out. Parker went into managing mode. "What's wrong? Did two dogs get in a fight? Is Keith okay? Are you okay? Was anyone attacked?"

Addy pulled up short and blinked. "No. No, the dogs are fine. Everyone is fine."

I wrinkled my brow as my annoyance went full tilt. "Then why the heck are you running out of the shelter like the hounds of hell on your trail? You scared the crap out of us."

Smooshie emphasized my claim by turning in two circles and pooping again near the last spot.

Addy seemed genuinely shaken, but CeCe looked almost as annoyed as me. She grabbed the dangling thing from Addy's hand and thrust it at me. "This is Tino's collar."

"Okay." The clasp on the small collar looked strange. Not something I'd seen before, but still, it was a collar. "Is it broken? We have some extras in the laundry room."

"It's not broken," CeCe said. "It's got a USB drive built into it."

"Really? That's a thing?" Parker asked.

"Yes, it is." CeCe's brow furrowed. "And the reason we're freaked out is because Addy decided it was a good idea to plug it in and take a look."

"And what was it?"

The teenager blushed. "You're just going to have to watch it yourself."

"Watch?" I turned to Parker. I could see he was thinking the same thing I was as he stripped the drive from CeCe grasp. "Thanks. We'll take a look."

"Watch" indicated video, and any video CeCe and Addy didn't want to talk about was probably a video I didn't want to see.

"Oh, no." My eyes widened.

"Yes," CeCe said. "There isn't enough eye bleach in all the world to erase what I saw. It was totally gross."

"How much did you watch?"

"Not much," Addy chimed in. "As soon as we knew what was happening, we turned it off."

My fear for Reggie heightened. "Did you…recognize anyone?"

"No," both teenagers said.

I breathed a sigh of relief. "You did the right thing, telling us about this."

Addy grinned as Tino whined and licked up the side of his face. "We better get this one to the backyard."

After the kids left, Parker turned to me. "We should turn this into the sheriff's department. Or at least to Nadine."

"You're right," I said. "But it's not that simple."

"Why? You're not on it, are you?" His crooked smile told me he wasn't serious.

"Now you're just being dumb." I shook my head. "Not me, but maybe a friend. I can't give that to the police until I know she's not on it." Even if I had to delete the evidence myself. That was the real difference between Shifters and humans. A Shifter's idea of justice was more primal and their loyalty fiercer. Human laws played in the shades of gray. Shifters saw things a lot more clearly.

Reggie hadn't killed Donnie.

And I wouldn't let her get nailed for it.

CHAPTER TWELVE

CONVINCING PARKER TO KEEP his dinner date with his dad had proven impossible. He canceled with Greer and then stood behind me in the shelter office as I opened the flash drive on the desktop computer. It had thirty-three .avi video files that were assigned numerical values only, which made it necessary to open each one. If I were honest with myself, I most likely would have opened each one out of morbid curiosity. Thirty-three files meant thirty-three suspects.

I watched several seconds of the first video as Donnie and a woman I didn't recognize tumbled into the bedroom. The angle was high and coming from the left. What was on the wall that could have hidden a camera?

The clock? Maybe. I blanched. "Do you think the camera is still in the room? I didn't see anything when I was there today." But maybe it saw me. I don't know how in the world I would explain that one to the sheriff.

"Today?" Parker asked.

"Uhm..." I pursed my lips. Looks like I wasn't keeping my little excursion to Doyle's house a secret. Or maybe Parker had the same effect on me that I had on other people—I didn't want to lie to him.

"I thought you were done with investigating. No more crime scenes for you."

"Well..." I shrugged.

Parker chuckled. "I never for one moment thought you'd actually stay out of this. It's not in your nature to stand on the sidelines."

I paused the video on the woman's face. "Do you recognize her?"

Parker shook his head. "No."

I clicked on the next file. Again, Donnie entered his bedroom with a woman. This one was shorter and curvier than the first woman. "What about her?"

Parker narrowed his gaze on the screen. "I think that's Della Thomas. Her folks used to run the feed store in town."

"Is she married?"

"I couldn't tell you. I haven't seen her in a couple of years. She hasn't changed much though."

I moved on to the next file. The scene was different. It was an office of some kind, and the camera was mobile. Donnie must have been holding it as he moved around the room.

"What are we looking at?" Parker asked.

"I'm not sure yet. There isn't anything to identify who the office belongs to."

"Could it be Doyle's home office?"

"No. I've been in there." Twice. "This isn't his home office."

The camera grazed past a window. "Pause it." Parker pointed to a building. "Isn't that Davis Auditorium?"

"You're right." Davis Auditorium was the college's gymnasium. "This office is in a building directly across from the front of the gym. What building is that?"

"You're asking the wrong guy. I've been to a couple of games at the auditorium, which is why I recognize it, but I don't spend much time at Two Hills Community College."

"We can ask Ryan."

"Why?"

"He works on campus, and he won't ask a lot of questions about why we want to know."

"Or we could just take a drive down to Two Hills."

"I thought you and Ryan were friends?"

"We are."

"You sure don't act like it."

"I don't like the way he acts around you."

"He's perfectly nice to me."

"Exactly. *Too* perfectly nice."

I laughed. "You know that Ryan Petry has zero interest in me."

Now Parker laughed…well, it was more like a "hah!" than a laugh. "He flirts with you constantly."

I shook my head. "Well, I'm not interested in him. That's all that should matter to you."

"Ryan has a way of turning a girl's head."

I stood up from the desk and put my palm on Parker's cheek. "You are the only man who turns my head."

He stared down at me, his blue eyes flickering between uncertainty and relief. "I don't think I could take it if it weren't true."

"It's true, Parker. I am only interested in you."

He leaned down and pressed his warm lips against mine. "Now that we've settled that, maybe we should call Ryan."

"Let's check these other files first."

"Who are you looking for?"

"I'd rather not say unless it ends up being necessary." I sat back down and unpaused the office video. Parker put his hand on my shoulder and leaned down to watch with me. We saw Donnie's face as he placed the camera at a high angle in the room that captured from the door to the desk. Donnie left the room, and the camera, after sixty seconds, turned off.

"That's weird." I clicked the next file. The video started with the door opening. Mr. Kirkshaw, the financial aid guy, and Ms. Lovell, my GED instructor, walked into the room. I stifled a gasp.

Parker's hand tightened on my shoulder. "You okay?"

"Yep." This wasn't the moment to tell him that I'd just seen the man this morning, and then spent seven hours with the woman. Besides, nothing was happening at this point except for some small talk about scheduling. "The camera seems to be motion-activated. I don't know why he'd save this though. It looks pretty harmless."

And then Ms. Lovell pulled down the shades.

"Uh oh."

"Things are about to heat up."

Ms. Lovell, who was such a nice lady, began kissing Mr. Kirkshaw, who was kind of yucky. Ew. "He's married," I said, remembering his wedding ring. "The home videos I could write off as something he did for private enjoyment, but this is too much. I think Donnie had to be blackmailing some of these people."

"Which is why we should stop watching and call Nadine at the very least," Parker said reasonably.

"Not yet." I wasn't turning anything over until I was certain Reggie wasn't implicated.

The next video made me blanch. "Crap."

"That's Lacy Evans."

"Yes, it is." I quickly moved on to the next. It was Rachel, the electronics lady from Walmart. As I made my way through more of the videos, I was disturbed by how many people I'd recognized, and I was only halfway through.

Parker squatted next to me. "Lily, you know I'm not going anywhere, so you might as well tell me who you think might be on here. Who are you protecting?"

"I'm hoping you will never have to know." He lightly pushed his elbow into my ribs. It tickled.

"You have a nice laugh."

"Thanks." I smiled as I clicked on the next file.

It was Parker's turn to say, "Crap." I paused on the brunette's face. "That's Jerry's wife, Shelly."

"No way." I recognized her as well. The woman from the bar who'd confronted Donnie after Rachel. "I saw her having an intense conversation with Donnie at Dally's. I had no idea she was Jerry's wife."

"You think he knows?"

"No, I don't. He talked about Donnie's reputation when he took me home last night, but he didn't act like a man scorned."

"These files are going to open a whole can of worms."

"I'd love to delete the entire thing, but someone killed Donnie Doyle, and that someone is probably in these files."

"Like your friend."

"She didn't do it."

He raised a brow but didn't say more on the subject.

After glimpsing the rest of the files, which ended up being more make-out movies, none of which were Reggie, I breathed a sigh of relief. I scooted back from the desk as Parker stood up and flexed his knees. "He didn't have a type, did he?" There were women of all ages, hair color, and build in those files.

"His type was female with a pulse," Parker said with a heavy dose of disgust. "How someone can do that to all those women, violate their privacy and trust, is beyond me. I'm surprised someone didn't kill him sooner." He rubbed his face as if he could scrub away all the awful he'd seen. "Can we call Nadine now?"

"Yes, now we call Nadine." Before I could take out my phone. Parker put his arms around me and kissed the top of my head. "What was that for?"

"I'm glad your friend wasn't on there."

I looked up at him, my chin resting on his chest. "Thanks. Me too."

*****

I met Nadine at The Cat's Meow. Parker stayed home with the dogs on the promise that I would return after with a double-bacon onion ring burger and a large order of steak fries for him.

My stomach dropped when I saw Reggie sitting with her in the corner booth. The diner was busy as Freda worked her way to each table, refilling tea and coffee as she went. She nodded as I passed her on my way to the table. "Lily," Nadine said enthusiastically. "How are you feeling?"

"Me?" I sat down on the same side as Reggie with my back to the crowded room and across from Nadine. "Why do you ask?" I worked to tune out all the conversations surrounding us so I could be present with my friends.

"You know…" she prodded. "The big day today. You were pretty bummed when you picked up Smooshie." She looked at Reggie. "She knows, right?"

"Knows what?" Reggie asked.

I waved my hand at Nadine. "I'm regretting telling you." I turned to Reggie. "I took my GED today at the college."

Reggie's frown disappeared. "That's so great! Why didn't you tell me earlier? I'm sure you aced it."

"I'm not confident. I'll probably have to take it again. I feel like I really blew the math and history parts. I'm pretty sure I got the year wrong for the War of 1812."

Nadine's mouth dropped open. "It's..."

"1812," Reggie and I said at the same time. We both laughed.

Nadine grinned and shook her head. "I meant it when I said you're one of the smartest people I know, but there is no sense worrying about how you did now. When do you get the results?"

"They said we will have the results on Monday."

"Two days." Nadine smiled. "That's not too bad."

"Two days of torture, you mean." I winked at her. Truth was, I hadn't really thought about the test since finding Reggie's earring. Nothing like a friend crisis to put your problems in perspective.

Freda carried a tray of food to the table. "One chicken salad." She slid that in front of Reggie. "One tenderloin with sweet potato fries." She slid that plate over to Nadine. I hadn't ordered yet, so I was surprised when she sat a heaping plate of food in front of me. "A lion special for Lily. A half-pound burger stuffed with pepper jack cheese, topped with double bacon, sharp cheddar, and lettuce, tomato, pickle chips, and jalapeno slices. Fries with the works." The works included chili, nacho cheese, bacon, and chives.

My stomach growled. "This is a fantasy plate right here."

"You can thank Buzz," Nadine said. "I told him you were coming for dinner, so he put it up with my order. He's been dying to try this one out on you."

Freda gave me a tight smile. "What can I get you to drink?"

"Sweet tea. Thanks, Freda."

She tucked her pad away in her pocket. "I'll be right back."

"Not that I'm not glad to see you, Lily, but you said you had something for me." Nadine stuffed a sweet potato fry in her mouth. "So, gimme."

I stole a glance at Reggie. "Addison and CeCe found this when they took the collar off Doyle's pup." I held out the collar.

"Does it have blood on it? Fingerprints? Is it a weapon? Help me out here, Lily. It looks like a small collar." Nadine took another bite of her fry.

I snapped the collar open, exposing the thumb drive. "It's more than that."

Nadine coughed, quickly chewed and swallowed. "Is that what I think it is?"

I leaned in close and lowered my voice. "If you think it's a storage drive full of incriminating videos, then yes, it's exactly what you think it is."

Reggie let out a soft "oh." I looked at her and shook my head. "I took a look because I wasn't sure what would be on there. It's not pretty. I recognized a few people, but nobody I know well."

Reggie's thin fingers trembled as she took a drink of her pop.

"Girl, are you okay?" Nadine asked Reggie. "You look like you swallowed a bug." Her eyes widened. She looked down at her plate then back up to our shaky friend. "You didn't swallow a bug, did you? Because I love that man in there, but I will not hesitate to shout bloody murder if he is serving insects on the side."

Reggie laughed nervously and patted her tightly coiffed hair. "No. No bug. But now that Lily has shared some surprising news about Donald Doyle, I guess it's my turn."

I held my breath, willing her to stay silent. It wasn't that I didn't think Nadine should know. On the contrary, as our friend, the cornerstone of our trio, she had to be told. But I also knew that once Nadine knew, she would have to report it to the sheriff. She had to choose her job. It was the right thing to do, but it didn't mean it wouldn't hurt Reggie.

"Did you find something when you examined him?" Nadine leaned forward with professional, yet eager curiosity.

Reggie's cheeks colored. "Not exactly. I've given the case to Dr. Azan, a medical examiner I studied under. He'll be down tomorrow to do the postmortem exam."

"On a Sunday," Nadine said. "That's dedication."

"He's a good friend." Reggie bowed her head.

"But why are you handing off the case?"

When Reggie didn't answer right away, I reached over and took her hand under the table and gave her a squeeze for courage.

Nadine placed her palms on the table. "Okay, you guys are fah-reak-ing me out. Just spill already."

"I can't do Donald Doyle's exam…" Reggie said, "…because I slept with him."

"What? How? Never mind how. When?"

Reggie teared up. "Last week on Tuesday, after the bar closed."

"How very interesting," a voice said behind me.

I felt my claws tear through the tips of my fingers and had to pull my hand from Reggie's.

Of all the people in the world to overhear our conversation, why did it have to be Naomi Freaking Wells?

CHAPTER THIRTEEN

I GAVE NADINE A "HOW COULD you not notice that my nemesis Naomi Wells had sat down in the booth behind us?" look.

My friend was already moving out of her seat to stand. Her voice was low, firm, and unfriendly. "You cannot report this, Naomi. Doyle's case is an open investigation."

Naomi raised her perfectly waxed eyebrow, her expression all cat-that-ate-the-canary. The contemptible woman stepped closer to Nadine, which put her right next to me. She spoke in the same quiet tones Nadine had adopted. "So you do think he was murdered?"

Nadine narrowed a steely gaze on the reporter. "I didn't say that. We're waiting for the postmortem."

"Which hasn't happened because the town coroner and medical examiner, it seems, is connected to the case...," she smiled, "...intimately."

Reggie turned ghost white as Naomi let the accusation drip from her lips like poison.

My predator roared to the surface, but I yanked her back. Luckily, my hands were on my lap and hidden by the table, otherwise everyone would've seen my claws. Once I got my temper under control, I put myself between Nadine and Naomi. I had to go up on my tiptoes to get close to her face. "What do you want?"

"You mean in exchange for forgetting this little conversation?" she asked. Triumph lit her mean gaze. "I think you know my price."

The knot in my stomach enlarged. I'd been warned by the prosecuting attorney not to discuss my witness statement for the Katherine Kapersky murder with anyone, but at this point, I was willing to do whatever it took to keep Reggie from the kind of humiliation a story in the *New St. Louis Dispatch* would bring. "Fine. I'll talk to you. And you'll never open your mouth about what you overheard today?" *Or I'll rip your face off*, I silently added.

She stared down at me, her blonde hair spilling over her slim shoulders. She smirked. "The only story I'm interested in is the one standing right in front of me." Naomi leaned sideways, not that she needed to since she towered over me by six or seven inches, to peek around me at Nadine. "It's so nice to see you, Deputy Booth." She nodded to Reggie. "Dr. Crawford."

*****

Reggie and Nadine left for the sheriff's station shortly after the Naomi fiasco. Nadine didn't want to take a chance that Naomi wouldn't keep her word. Reggie needed to make an official statement before Naomi could break her promise. I wanted to go along, for moral support, but Nadine pointed out that my presence wouldn't make the sheriff feel any kindlier toward Reg. She wasn't wrong. The sheriff saw me as an antagonist in the story of his life.

As I left The Cat's Meow, movement near my truck put me on high alert. I let the paper sack with Parker's dinner sag next to my thigh. If I needed to drop the meal, doing it from that height would give it the best chance to survive any strange encounters.

I let my cougar slip forward into my eyes and the darkness abated. The figure was a man, medium build, and in his thirties. I didn't recognize him.

I made my voice a growl as I loudly asked, "Who are you and why are you skulking around my truck?"

The guy stepped off the pavement and onto the sidewalk, effectively blocking my way to the driver's side door. "Give it to me," he demanded. He reached out with trembling hands, his heart beating so loud I could hear it with my sensitive ears.

"I don't know what you're talking about. Right now, we can chalk this up to a mistake on your part, but if you don't leave me alone, I *will* hurt you."

He took a step toward me then hesitated. "Your eyes," he said. "What's wrong with your—"

A speedy blur crashed into the man and knocked him to the ground.

Uncle Buzz was on top of the man, his knees on the guy's shoulders, his arm raised and his hand balled up into a fist. Hair had sprouted on my arms during the quick encounter, but Buzz still looked completely human. No fur, no fangs, no claws, and his eyes were one-hundred percent non-feline. I guess it was the difference between living with normals for forty years versus one year. Buzz was a cool customer. Still, he'd moved with Shifter speed. That would be something he wouldn't want to explain.

I looked around the parking lot. A few people had gathered outside the diner's door. Goddess in a box, this might get ugly if anyone was taking video. I forced my inner animal to calm down. But seeing a gun next to the man made it a much more difficult task. I sucked in a breath.

"It's all right, Lils," Buzz said. He pushed the gun a few feet from the now crying man. What in all the levels of hell was this guy's problem?"

I turned to the crowd once my mundane night vision returned. "Someone call the police." I knelt down next to Buzz and the stranger. I looked at the man, who I could see now had light brown hair and hazel eyes.

He blinked up at me. "I'm sorry. I wasn't going to hurt you, I swear it."

"Is that true?" I put a lot of power into my words. "You didn't plan to hurt me?"

"Only if you wouldn't give me the flash drive. It was a last resort."

"Uh huh." My stomach clenched, and I felt like throwing up. I'd grown up in a dangerous world of magic and werecreatures who liked to fight and kill as much as anyone else, but I'd never even seen a gun until I'd moved to Moonrise, and to date, I'd been shot at three times. Anger overrode my fear. "Who are you, and why did you want the drive?"

"My wife," the man said. "She told me…she told me what Doyle did to her. He raped her, and he filmed it. I can't let anyone see what he did to her. It would destroy her."

More likely it would destroy *him*. My mojo was in high gear, so I knew the man believed what he was saying. The problem was if his wife was one of the many women on the drive, she'd lied to him. There wasn't a single woman who hadn't been a willing bedmate. "What's your name?"

"Richard O'Reilly," he said.

"O'Reilly Florist Shop," Buzz said.

"My mother's business," Richard replied. "I work at the bank." He shook his head. "Give me the drive. Or better yet, destroy it."

I could hear sirens before I saw the lights.

"I'm sorry, Richard. It's too late. I already gave the memory stick to a deputy."

A choking sob forced its way from his chest. I looked at Buzz. He frowned and shook his head. I knew he wanted me to keep my mouth shut. Poor deluded man.

"Is that why you killed Donnie?" I asked.

"What?" He blinked up at me, surprise clear on his face. "I didn't—"

"All right folks, clear off," I heard Deputy Bobby Morris say to the diner crowd. "Either go back inside or leave." There was a lot of murmuring as they dispersed.

Bobby stood over us from the sidewalk. "What's going on, Ms. Mason? Buzz?"

"Richard here tried to attack my cousin," Buzz said. "I saw he had a gun and tackled him to the ground."

The deputy leaned forward. "Richard O'Reilly? What in the world?"

"You know him?" I asked.

"Yes," Bobby said. "Richard's wife is Rita, the evidence-room clerk."

"Nadine has something you all are going to want to see before you let her come back to work."

Richard sobbed again. I didn't have the heart to tell him the truth about his wife. But how in the world did anyone know I had the flash drive?

Bobby secured Richard's gun, then got the man up from the ground and put him in handcuffs. He looked at Buzz and me. "You two are going to have to come down and give a statement."

"Great. I can't wait." I looked back at the dropped dinner bag. "Can I make a quick detour first?"

"Give us an hour," Buzz said. "I've got to get the diner closed out before I can head over."

Bobby nodded. "See you then."

I picked up my sack. Buzz put his arm around my shoulder and walked me to my driver door. "You going to be okay, kid?" The way he said it, the tone, even his expression, reminded me so much of my dad. And at that moment, the grief of his death hit me all over again.

I teared up. "Thanks for being here for me tonight."

"You'd have handled it," he said, but not in a way that made me believe him.

"Well, I'm glad I didn't have to handle it."

"By the way, that's some trick you've got there." He raised his brows, his green eyes staring into my soul.

"What trick?" I wasn't dumb, but maybe he was talking about something other than my ability to get people to tell the truth.

"How did you do it? How did you get him to say all that?"

"It's a long story," I told him. "One for another night when Parker's dinner isn't cooling ten degrees every minute."

"But you will tell me?"

I smiled. "Cross my heart."

CHAPTER FOURTEEN

THE HAIR ON THE BACK of my neck stood at attention while I waited for Bobby to take my statement. According to Deputy Janet Larimore, a large, confident brunette, Bobby was still processing his earlier arrest. I yawned as I sat next to his desk in the witness-slash-perp chair. It had been an early morning for me. Still, I was grateful for the late hour. It meant Sheriff Avery had already clocked out for the day, and I wouldn't have to deal with his suspicious, probing questions. The man liked to probe so much he could give a proctologist a run for his money.

Parker, who shared my concern about Avery, had offered to go to the station with me, but Elvis had been particularly clingy when he was saying the words. The dog could sense Parker's deep anxiety related to the sheriff's department. I didn't blame him. He'd been locked up for several days in the jail, and it had placed a real strain on him.

Smooshie had wanted to go with me. I think she was ready for one of our nightly runs, but I wasn't going home, and while it wasn't hot this evening, it was unseasonably warm. I had no idea how long it would take to give my statement, and I didn't want my baby girl waiting in the truck the whole time.

Nadine had texted right before I'd arrived that she and Reggie were done at the station. I don't know if Buzz told her about the guy who tried to attack me. Since my new phone wasn't blowing up, I guessed probably not. I stretched as I yawned again. I don't like to think of myself as impatient or irritable in general, but I felt both as I waited on Bobby Morris. I was ready to be home in my own bed, snuggled down with my Smooshie girl, and done with this whole awful business.

And then I saw it...

Donald Doyle's file was in the tray on Bobby's desk.

It was as if the Fates, who I'd heard were horrible creatures, were testing my resolve. *I will not peek,* I repeated several times in my head.

There was a piece of paper sticking slightly past the opening in the manila folder. Maybe I should just tuck it in. After all, the way it was placed, it could easily fall out and then some key piece of the investigation might be lost forever. Even to myself that last part of my thought process had come off as lame. But still, it was my civic duty to help the police when possible. That was my story, and I was sticking to it.

I reached out and flicked the file where the paper was out, and—not unpredictably—the entire folder slid out of the bin and spilled onto Bobby's desk. I looked around to see if anyone had noticed.

Nope. No one. Larimore was on the far side of the room with her head behind a computer monitor, pecking away at her keyboard, and totally not paying attention to me. Once again, the Fates were rearing their ugly heads. I used a pencil, eraser side down, to move the papers out in a way that I could see what was on them.

A small handwritten note, the words written in big, bold letters, caught my attention right away.

I saw what you did. I am watching you.

Goddess. Was this note written by Doyle? Had he been the poison pen all along?

My stomach churned. He had lived less than a mile from my place. What if he'd seen me change into my other form? What if he'd taken video of my transformation? What if...

Oh, crap. The empty drive cap. What if he had something incriminating on me that the killer took from Doyle's office?

I took a deep breath to steady my racing pulse. No. I had been staying in the apartment over Parker's garage when I received my own poison-pen note. I wasn't even on Donnie Doyle's radar at that time. It couldn't have been him. But maybe Donnie had gotten a letter, too. And that meant someone probably knew what he was doing.

"What in Sam Hell are you doing, Ms. Mason?"

I'd been so distracted by my fear of what Donnie might have on me, that I hadn't noticed the clomping hooves of the overweight Sheriff Avery.

"I...nothing." I tried to scoot the chair back from the desk, only to discover it was bolted to the floor. I glanced guiltily at the folder. "I accidentally knocked the file over. I didn't want to touch it, you know, just in case there was, er, something in there I shouldn't touch."

Sheriff Avery honest-to-goodness growled at me, and for a second there, it was old home week. He'd made a noise so rumbly it would have made a werewolf proud. "I need you to get up, Ms. Mason, and step away from Deputy Morris' desk. Now."

I stood up and took a giant sidestep away from the desk and the sheriff. He smelled like alcohol that had been set on fire and put out with garbage. Blech. He straightened the folder and put it back in the tray, all the while mumbling harshly under his breath about pain-in-the-butt women, and I'm paraphrasing here, and how he had half a mind to arrest me for being a nuisance.

"You're right about the half a mind," I muttered, too low for him to really hear.

Sheriff Avery turned his sharp gaze on me. "Did you say something, Ms. Mason?"

The sheriff's hearing had been better than I thought. Oops. A familiar face walked through a door on the far side of the room. "There's Deputy Morris." I turned to the sheriff. "Once I make my statement, I'll get out of your hair."

"The only way you could get out of my hair is if you moved to another county." And with that grouchy statement, the sheriff headed toward his office.

Morris sat down in his chair, his eyes tired as he glanced my way.

"You arrived in the nick of time," I told him.

"What's the sheriff doing back in the station?" Bobby asked.

"Your guess is as good as mine," I told him.

Nadine and Buzz arrived just as I finished writing down everything I could remember about the incident in the diner parking lot, minus all Shifter stuff. Richard was too messed up to even notice anything paranormal. I really felt for the guy—especially when he found out that his wife was a willing participant in Donnie's bed.

Larimore got up to open the locked front door. She ushered in a thin, wispy woman with short blonde hair. I recognized her as one of Donnie's lovers from the drive. She said to the deputy, "This is all a misunderstanding."

I glanced at Buzz, raising my brows. He gave a slight shake of his head. I turned to Bobby. "Do you need anything else from me?"

"Not tonight," the man said. He gave me a crooked smile. "Try not to trip over any bodies on the way home."

"That's not funny."

He smirked and shrugged. "It kind of is."

Across the room, I heard Nadine talking in low tones to Larimore. Larimore told her that the sheriff wasn't happy about the USB discovery, and he'd come in to view the new evidence for himself. Larimore also told her that she recognized one of the women on the videos as the sheriff's niece, Rachel Keeton.

Crap on toast. Poop was about to hit the fan. "Okay, well, I'll see you later, Deputy Morris."

I grabbed my purse and hauled my butt toward the door. Buzz took my arm. "Did you hear what that deputy told Nadine?"

"Why do you think I'm leaving so fast? I'm sure if Sheriff Avery can find a way, he'll arrest me for his niece's indiscretion. Depending on how fast he watches all the files, I'd say you probably have five minutes before this place blows up. You should hurry up and make your statement."

Buzz shook his head and gave me a half smile. "Avery doesn't dislike me the way he dislikes you."

"Let's face it. The man hates me. Which is why I'm leaving. Call me tonight after you're done here."

Nadine approached me after Buzz made his way to Morris' desk, her face somber and serious.

"How's Reggie?" I asked.

"She's upset about the whole thing. I'm glad she wasn't on the drive, but damn, those poor women."

Reggie wouldn't have been on the drive even if she *had* been on it, because friends don't let friends go down like that. But I agreed with Nadine's sentiment. "Do you have to work now? Or are you here for Buzz?"

"Both. Avery has found a way to blame me for the late discovery of the evidence and for not notifying him sooner about Reggie's involvement."

"That's a bunch of bull! You didn't find out about any of it until tonight."

"You're acting like the sheriff is a reasonable human being."

"Man, Nadine. I'm sorry."

"For what? Bringing us the drive is the first real lead we have." She looked at the sheriff's closed door. "Now get on out of here while you can. I'll call you when I know anything new."

*****

By the time I picked up Smooshie and got her home, I was completely exhausted. Shifters have a lot of energy and stamina, but the lack of sleep had taken its toll on me. Smooshie danced around me when we got out of the truck.

"Sorry, girl." I scratched her ear. "Not tonight." I put the key in the trailer door and turned it, but it was still locked. "Dang. I really am tired." I tried again, and this time it opened. "Come on, Smoosh. Let's get to bed."

My adorable pittie whacked her tail against my legs several times then headed to the back of the trailer to our bedroom. I yawned deeply, suddenly even more tired than before. This had been a day from hell. First, probably blowing my GED, then finding out about Reggie and the drive, confronting the attacker—all of it had drained my energy. I wasn't sure I could take any more. I stretched, shedding clothes on my way through the kitchen area into the narrow hallway, past the tiny bathroom, until I collapsed on the bed next to Smooshie.

She crawled toward me, planting her elbows and paws on my back. "Off, Smoosh," I mumbled. My voice sounded weird, almost hollow. Smooshie began to lick my ear. I tried to push her away, but my arms felt leaden. "Stah—op," I slurred.

Smooshie barked and whined. *Why won't she stop licking my face?* Did she have to potty? She'd just gone both number one and number poo at Parker's right before we'd left. I giggled at my play on words. "Number pooo," I said.

Something wasn't right.

Smooshie nudged me with her big head, pushing against me until I forced my legs to move. I slowly rolled out of bed, but when I tried to stand, I collapsed to the floor.

My faithful companion jumped down in front of me. She barked, but it was more like a cough. Whatever had affected me was affecting her as well. My skin had turned a bright shade of pink.

Pink skin, lethargy, drowsiness. Symptoms. Of what? My brain felt foggy. I knew what this was. This was…

Smooshie had gotten behind me and was now pushing me forward. I couldn't keep my feet, so I dropped to my knees and crawled toward the back door.

Carbon monoxide poisoning.

The sudden, awful thought gave me a small jolt of adrenaline. I got to the door, reached up to unlock it, and shoved it open. Smooshie and I tumbled out into the fresh air. Why in the heck hadn't the carbon monoxide detector gone off? If the concentrations were high enough to affect me, they were high enough to set off the alarm.

After several minutes of deep breathing and wishing like hell I hadn't taken all my clothes off, I held my breath, ran back inside and grabbed my robe and my phone, then headed back out with Smooshie. Also, I noted the carbon monoxide detector dangling on the wall, the battery missing from its slot.

I punched the all-too-familiar numbers into my phone.

"Nine-one-one, what's your emergency?" the switchboard operator answered.

"Please send a deputy," I said. "I think someone just tried to kill me."

CHAPTER FIFTEEN

THE POLICE, THE FIRE department, and the paramedics tramped around my property. There was so much flash and color it looked like a county event.

I called Parker for moral support and Ryan Petry for Smooshie. I needed the vet to make sure she was okay. The sweet baby, once again, had saved my life.

A paramedic named Robyn, with short, tight curly hair and beautiful dark skin, put an oxygen monitor on my index finger and an oxygen mask over my nose and mouth. She was as short as me, but with a better, more feminine figure. "Breath deep," she told me. The redness in my skin had already disappeared, and while I had a headache, I didn't feel tired anymore.

I watched Parker rush past the fire truck to get to me. He stopped just short of the gurney Robyn had insisted I get on. "Is she all right?" he asked the paramedic. "Are you taking her to the hospital?"

I lifted the mask from my face. "She can talk."

Robyn shoved the mask back down. "No, she can't."

I grabbed Parker's hand and lifted the mask again, but not so far off my face. "Get Smooshie," I said. "She's over there with Jerry." Jerry had kindly taken responsibility for her so that the paramedics could do their job and also keep her out of the way for the firefighters. "Ryan is on his way to check her out."

I was proud of Parker for not even looking the tiniest bit jealous. Instead, he went into "I've got a purpose" mode and made a beeline for Jerry and Smooshie.

"That your fella?" Robyn asked.

I nodded, even though we hadn't even had our first date. He was mine, and that was that.

"Bravo," she said, a slow smile spreading across her lips as she gave him a cursory glance. "Brah-vo."

"What in tarnation have you gotten into now?" asked the less-than-sympathetic voice of Sheriff Avery. "I swear I'm going to have to hire new deputies just to keep up with all your shenanigans. What do you have to say for yourself?"

I sighed and pointed to my mask. When he narrowed his suspicious gaze at me, I shrugged. If I wasn't allowed to talk to Parker because I needed the oxygen, then I certainly wouldn't break the rule for this jerk. He opened his mouth to protest, but Robyn, my new knightess in shining armor, stepped in.

"You're going to have to ask your questions later, Sheriff. Right now, the patient needs oxygen. Carbon monoxide poisoning is very serious. I'm sure you don't want to be responsible for any lasting damage Ms. Mason suffers."

Avery's face went a dark purple color. "Now you just wait a minute…"

"Sheriff!" Bobby Morris shouted. "The fire chief needs to talk to you."

That was something I did want to hear. I tuned out the running engines and extraneous chatter and dialed into the conversation between the fire chief and the sheriff.

"The levels in the house were twenty times the normal limit, and that's with Ms. Mason leaving the door open after she exited."

"Is that a lot?" the sheriff asked. I could hear the incredulity in the chief's voice.

"Yes, it's a lot."

"Any chance it's an accident?"

Well, I knew that someone had taken the battery out of the carbon monoxide detector, and, I suspect, that my mishap with the front door, locking it when I turned the key, was because the door had been unlocked. I'd look for tool marks in the keyhole when all this was over.

"A rag blocked the vent to the furnace, and it didn't just stuff itself in there. Someone did this on purpose."

"Could be attempted suicide. Maybe she changed her mind."

"Well, that's for you to find out, Mike. My job is to investigate the cause and determine if it's an accident or a crime. It's a crime. That's your territory."

"You're awfully testy tonight, Lloyd."

"It's my wedding anniversary."

Avery laughed. "Once a year whether you deserve it or not, right?"

I groaned at the implied nod-and-wink then tuned the two men out as they jabbered about things that didn't apply to me.

Ryan Petry pulled up in his sports car. Ouch, my gravel road probably gave that fancy little thing a beating. He popped the trunk, ran around to the back, and grabbed a bag and a small tank. He didn't stop to check on me. Instead, he made directly for Smooshie, and I swear I never liked the man more. After Ryan went to work on my dog, who really didn't seem worse for wear, Parker joined me at the ambulance.

I pushed the mask away. "What's Ryan say? Is Smooshie going to be all right?"

"I'm about to glue that thing to your face. You're going to look really funny walking around with a rubber mask as a permanent fixture," Robyn said.

I snapped it back into place and gave her a quick salute before pressing Parker for information with a "hurry up and tell me" stare.

"You've got about a minute to wrap this up before I take you to the hospital," Robyn added. "So make it quick."

After she walked around to the front of her rig, Parker blew out a breath. "She's a hard taskmaster."

I nodded. My headache was almost gone now, and the nausea had disappeared shortly after she'd put me on straight oxygen. I took Parker's hand. "Will you keep Smooshie?" I asked.

"I'll go with Ryan and stay with her until we get the blood test results to see if she still has carbon monoxide in her blood." He laced his fingers with mine. "Every part of me wants to be with you tonight, but I know you won't be able to sit still and let the doctors do what they have to do to check you out if I don't take care of Smooshie first."

Smart man. I smiled, though I'm not sure he could see it through the mask. I squeezed his hand.

"How does this work, with, you know, your special condition?"

By condition, he meant the fact that I turned into a cougar sometimes. I'd read somewhere that animals are even more susceptible to carbon monoxide poisoning, so I'm not sure if it would be worse for me than a normal human. I guess I was about to find out.

Robyn rounded the corner with her driver, a paramedic named Steve. "Time to go, lovebirds." She and Steve pushed the gurney into the back of the ambulance, and the wheels folded up as I slid inside. Robyn got in beside me. I picked my head up and gave Parker one last look before Steve closed the doors behind us.

Why would someone try to poison me? It made zero sense. I didn't have the drive anymore. It was already with the cops, so what did killing me accomplish?

Then another thought occurred to me. What if this incident had nothing to do with my involvement in Donnie Doyle's case?

*****

I shared the emergency room with a crying baby, an elderly woman who kept shouting, "help me," and a college student suffering from alcohol poisoning. A lab technician came in and took several vials of my blood. She got into my vein quick and with hardly any pain. My lucky night, except for the attempt on my life, of course.

A lanky man with a white lab coat, a stethoscope sticking out of his front pocket, and holding a chart, presumably mine, walked into my room. "I'm Dr. Wilkens," he said. "What seems to be the trouble tonight?"

I wanted to point out that he was holding all my information in his hot little hands, but I played nice. "I inhaled a bunch of carbon monoxide."

"How do you feel right now?"

"A little light-headed, which is probably due to all the oxygen they've been pumping into me tonight…" I tapped the plastic oxygen tube poking in my nose, "…but otherwise, not bad."

He pulled the stethoscope from his pocket and placed it in his ears. "Lean forward," he directed. He placed the cold disc end against my chest. "Take a deep breath for me?" I did. He moved it around and made the same request five more times. He stood up straight, nodding his head as he put the stethoscope back in his pocket. "Nice and clear. Yep, I think you're gonna be just fine." He smiled reassuringly. "I'll be back when the test results are in, but I think you'll get to go home tonight."

"Thanks, Doc. Do you think I could get my robe? The nurse put it somewhere when she made me put on this gown." My cell phone was in my robe pocket, and I wanted to call Parker.

"I'll send in Judy to help you out." He exited the room, while I played the game of hurry up and wait.

The baby finally stopped crying, poor thing. The elderly woman still occasionally belted out, "help me."

Then I heard a familiar voice say, "Buzz Mason, what are you doing here?"

"I'm visiting my cousin. She was brought in here tonight. What are you doing here, Opal? Everything all right?"

"Pearl's taken a turn. This is the second time in the past year." I'd never heard the bold, elderly woman ever sound so…defeated.

"She'll bounce back," my uncle said. "She always does."

"Until she doesn't," Opal said. "You better go find Lily."

Then I heard another familiar voice. "Hey, Buzz." The sultry sounds came from none other than Lacy Evans. I just couldn't get away from that girl. "How you doing?"

"Is Freda sick?" Buzz asked.

"No. It's Paulie. He started running a fever tonight, high enough that he had a seizure. They got it down to something manageable now, but they want to keep him for a while for observation."

"Do you want me to call Freda?"

"No," Lacy said. "I've got this."

The conversation trailed off from there. Was Lacy really getting her life together? I mean, I still saw her out drinking on Tuesday nights, but she had sat for the GED just like me, and she hadn't made her mom handle her kid's crisis. Hell, she'd even thanked me for stepping in when Jock had been coming on strong. Maybe a leopard really could change its spots.

Judy, the nurse, came back into my room and handed me a plastic sack with my robe in it. "Buzz Mason is here to see you. He says he's family, so I let him come back, but if you want me to send him out to the waiting room, I will."

I gave her a half smile. "It's okay to let him in."

She poked her head out of the doorway. "Come on back!"

Buzz arrived and stood next to my bed, his gaze filled with concern.

"I'll give you two a little privacy while we're waiting for your results," said Judy. She closed the door behind her.

Buzz held out a plastic shopping sack. "Nadine got these from your place after the fire department said it was safe to go inside. It's some jeans, a shirt, and some undergarments. She said you'd need them."

"That girl of yours is super smart." I gratefully took the sack from him. "I don't suppose she put a toothbrush and some toothpaste in there?" I must have puked after I stumbled out of the trailer because my mouth tasted disgusting.

"It's in there. Along with a hairbrush."

I grinned. "She's a keeper."

"For as long as she'll have me," Buzz replied. "Now, what in the hell happened out there?"

I knew Nadine had probably given him the official version, but I broke it down with theatrics and all. I told him how heroic Smooshie had been. "She saved my life, Buzz." Tears blurred my vision. "She saved me."

My uncle sat on the side of my bed and put his arm around my shoulders and pulled me into him. "She's earned herself a free beef patty every day for the rest of her life."

"She's on a diet," I sniffled.

Buzz chuckled. "Fine, then I'll give her grilled chicken breast instead."

"Perfect."

A loud commotion out in the hall got our attention. Buzz went to the door and opened it.

We heard Lacy screaming then a man yelled, "You're fired! Don't bother picking up your last paycheck, you blackmailing bitch."

And then we heard a gunshot.

CHAPTER SIXTEEN

BUZZ SLAMMED THE DOOR SHUT.

I scrambled from the bed.

"What do you think you're doing?" Buzz asked.

"Getting dressed so we can go kick butt." I gave him a side-eyed glance as I dumped the contents of Nadine's bag on the bed and dressed. "We have skills that normal humans don't. We have a responsibility to help."

"We have a responsibility to keep Shifters secret, and that ain't going to happen if we go all furry every time there's trouble."

Buzz didn't seem to believe his own words. I could see his troubled expression. Like my dad, he wasn't the kind of person who could let bad things happen to good people.

"Opal, Pearl, and Lacy are out there. And a bunch of innocent people."

"We're not superheroes," he protested.

"Yes, we are." I pushed past him to my room's door and cracked it open. It had gone mostly quiet out there. I could hear a few whispers, but even with my Shifter hearing, I couldn't make out the words.

I peeked out and scanned the nurses' station then looked down the short hallway toward the security door that led to the waiting room. Dr. Wilkens, Nurse Judy, and some other people in peach and blue scrubs were all on the ground. Lacy was flattened against the wall.

But the big surprise was Opal, holding a small gun over a terrified Jock Simmons as dust from a damaged ceiling tile fell down around her head. How in the heck had he gotten past the security door?

I stepped out of the room. "Opal," I said. "I'm coming over to you. Okay?"

She kept her fixed gaze on Jock. "Someone needs to take out this piece of trash."

"It shouldn't be you, though. Pearl needs you. You're no good to her in jail."

I was only ten feet away now. She kept the gun pointed at Jock with her right hand and gently touched her cheek with her left. Her fingers trembled. "No man should ever hit a woman."

"You're right," I told her. I looked at Lacy again. She had a red mark rising on her cheek. Jock must have punched her, and that action had triggered a reaction in Opal that the man might not live to regret.

I'd suspected for a while that Jock beat his wife, and him hitting Lacy confirmed he was capable of being that kind of monster. As far as I was concerned, Jock's demise would be a service to womankind everywhere.

"The police will arrest him for assault," Buzz said as he finally joined me. "You can't take the law into your own hands. Lily's right. Pearl needs her sister."

I looked around the room of cowering people. "You're frightening the doctors and nurses, Opal. They can't take care of your sister if they're scared."

Jock whimpered. "You're crazy, lady!" This close, I could smell the bourbon weeping from his pores.

I saw the look in Opal's eyes. It was one that I'd seen before back home. This was a woman who was prepared to take action.

"I'd shut my mouth if I were you," I told him. "I don't think Opal will hesitate to shoot you given the right motivation."

Her finger hugged the trigger. "Just give me a reason," she told him. "I would love to blow your head off."

The emergency room doors opened. Sheriff Avery walked in with Deputy Larimore at his hip. He had his weapon drawn. "Put the gun down, Ms. Dixon."

"Jock came in looking for a fight," I said. "Opal was just defending Lacy Evans."

"I'll handle this, Ms. Mason. When you get involved, people die."

Ouch. My heart actually skipped a beat.

"That's not fair, Sheriff," Buzz said. "Lily hasn't done anything wrong. Hell, she's kept Opal from killing the son-of-a-bitch. You should be thanking her, not blaming her."

The sheriff ignored Buzz, his gun still trained on the elderly spinster. Naomi Wells appeared from down the hall. I groaned. Goddess, I couldn't get away from this woman!

"Senior Citizen Gunned Down by County Sheriff for Defending Young Woman from Drunk," she said, using her hands to emphasize each word. "It'll make a great headline, don't you think?"

The sheriff hesitated then lowered his gun. "Now, there is no need for this to escalate." He pointed to Jock. "If you put your gun down, Ms. Dixon, I can let my deputy arrest Jock."

"There's only one way to fix a man this broken," Opal said, but she dropped her hand to her side, the gun now pointing at the tiled floor. "But I suppose it isn't my job to take on." She stared at Jock. "I see you. The whole town sees you. You better smarten up."

Avery slowly walked to Opal and took her pistol while Larimore picked Jock up from the floor and put him in handcuffs. "I'm going to have to take you down to the station, Ms. Dixon. You discharged a firearm inside a hospital, and I'm sorry, but I have to do it."

Opal nodded. "Let me just say goodbye to Pearl."

I rushed over the Lacy. He cheek was starting to puff up. "Let's get you checked out. You might have a fracture. You'll need an X-ray to make certain."

"I'm okay," she said.

"What happened? Why did Jock attack you?"

"It's so stupid. I got mad. You know how he's been harassing me. So, I told him I was going to report him to the state bar association if he didn't give me a raise and stop messing with me." She touched her swollen face. "I didn't think he'd do this. Thanks, Lily. Thank you." A choking noise emanated from her throat and tears streamed down her cheeks.

"What, no thanks for me?" Naomi asked. "Nothing like a little threat to put the sheriff in his place." She smiled as if I should be happy she showed up. I wasn't.

A nurse came and took Lacy. I glared at Naomi. "What are you doing here? Did someone tell you I was here? And what? You thought you would come down and get the scoop?"

Naomi flushed guiltily. Calmly, she said, "That's exactly why I'm here. Who tried to kill you, Lily? Why are you a target?"

"The only person who seems to have it out for me is you," I hissed.

"Well, I can always run with my back-up story. You know, the one about the local medical examiner sleeping with the victim of a murder, a man half her age at that."

"You promised."

"I promised I wouldn't run it if you let me interview you."

"And I will, about the Tom Jones case, not about this one."

"You'll talk about whatever case I want to talk about, or your friend will have to learn to live with the public humiliation."

"We had a deal, Naomi."

Naomi smirked. "I'm changing the deal."

"You really suck, you know that."

She grinned, and it was more feral than a Shifter's. "I do know it."

Buzz interrupted us, and probably a good thing because I was about to go all fur and claws on Naomi. "The doctor wants to talk to you about your test results."

"This isn't over," Naomi said.

"I couldn't agree more," I replied. Buzz put his arm around my shoulder, and we went back to the room.

"Didn't Jock call Lacy out for being a blackmailer before Opal stepped in?" I asked Buzz when we were safely away from my nemesis.

"Yep." He shook his head. "That girl is going to be the death of her mom. Freda is at the end of her wits."

I didn't tell him about Lacy taking the GED exam. One, it wasn't my news to share, and two, it seemed inappropriate given everything that had happened in the corridor. "Donnie Doyle was a blackmailer."

"Was he?" Buzz acted disinterested.

"You don't think that's a coincidence, do you?"

"It's not our concern. You asked me once how I managed to live among humans for so long, and I told you then like I'm telling you now—I mind my own business. That's the only way we survive out here, away from our own kind." He wrapped his arms around me. "I've lost my brother, you lost your dad, your mom, and your sibling. We are all we have left of Mason family. I can't lose you, Lily." He let me go and held me out at arm's length. "But, you seem bound and determined to put yourself in harm's way. I want to lock you in a cellar somewhere for your own good."

"But you wouldn't, right?" Shifters could be literal sometimes, but I was pretty sure Buzz didn't mean it.

"Keep putting yourself in danger, and you'll find out." The corner of his mouth tugged up in a half-smile.

"I thought the doctor was coming to give me lab results."

"I lied," he said. "I was worried you were going to eat a certain annoying reporter if I didn't intervene."

"Valid," I told him. "Although, I probably would have to spit her out. I prefer my food less rotten."

Buzz chuckled. "I find it hard to believe you'd spit any food out. I mean, I know we have a fast metabolism, but you eat even more than I do."

"I'm a growing girl!" Speaking of growing girls. I pulled my robe from the bag the nurse had brought in and found my phone. "I need to make a quick call."

Buzz sat in the visitor chair in the room. "Tell Parker hi for me."

I rolled my eyes. I brought up my contacts and clicked to call. Parker answered on the first ring.

"Are you okay? What's the doctor say? Are you going to be admitted? How are you feeling?"

"Uhm, how's Smooshie?"

"She's great. Ryan said her the carbon monoxide levels in her blood were low. She got lucky. He put her in an oxygen tent, and he wants to keep her in there for a few more hours."

A rush of relief infused me. I had to fight not to cry. I don't know what I would have done if Smooshie had been really hurt. Maybe Buzz was right, and I had brought this on myself. I could have stayed out of Doyle's mess. I could have not gone to his house and found his body. And even though I told myself I would stay out the investigation, I had gone out of my way to investigate. "I'm so glad. Hug her for me, and tell Ryan thank you." I sat on the bed. "And Parker, thank you. I don't know if I could get through this without you."

"Sure you would, Lils. You're the strongest person I know."

"Awww." His praise made me feel warm and fuzzy. "Is Greer with Elvis? Do you need to be with Elvis?"

He knew what I was asking him. Was his PTSD kicked into high gear because of me? "Ryan has all kinds of fur-kids in his kennels for me to pet, and dad is taking good care of Elvis for me. I want to be here for you and Smooshie. Don't worry about me. Just take care of yourself." He paused for a second. "Lily, when they discharge you, I want you to come stay at my place. You can have the room over the garage again, or you can take the spare bedroom in my house. Whatever you want."

"Why, Parker Knowles," I said coyly. "Are you asking me to move in with you?"

He stammered, and I laughed.

"I'm just teasing you. I know it's a temporary offer."

"The offer stands for as long as you're willing to stay." And with that response, he hung up on me.

I must have had a stunned look on my face because my uncle busted out in a belly laugh. "You look like the cat that got ate by the canary."

"Ha, ha. Laugh it up."

"So, you planning on taking the boy's offer to shack up? In the short term, I'm all for it. It's a nicer alternative to locking you in the basement."

"Shack up?" Goddess take my breath, had Parker really just asked me to move in with him? "I'm pretty sure we should get through our first date before he hands me the keys to his kingdom."

The doctor came in and interrupted us. "I've got the results," he said. "Do you want the good news or the bad news?"

"Just the news, Doc. Good and bad."

"The good news is that you're not pregnant."

I raised a brow at him.

"Just a joke," he said. "We did have to run a pregnancy test though, they're standard for carbon monoxide poisoning. The good news is that you aren't showing any severe symptoms from your exposure. No dementia, seizures, and your lungs are clear. However, your blood work still shows high levels of carbon monoxide in your system. We're going to keep you overnight on oxygen and monitor your progress. I'm confident you'll be able to leave in the morning."

"Okay," I said, wishing there was a witch healer in town. The one back home could have gotten me out of here tonight. Human medicine was much slower. I turned to Buzz. "You should go home. That diner of yours doesn't open itself in the mornings."

"I don't want to leave you alone."

"This hospital is full of people. I won't be alone," I told him. "Go. Get some sleep. I'll see you tomorrow."

Buzz stood up and kissed my forehead. "Get well and try to stay out of trouble tonight."

"Trouble finds me," I told him. No three words spoken had ever been so true.

CHAPTER SEVENTEEN

THE BEEPING OF MONITORS in the intensive care unit kept me half-awake most of the night. That, and I found it difficult to sleep with plastic tubes sticking in my nose. Plus, the dry oxygen had started to irritate my nostrils. The nurses came in every hour to check my pulse oxygen with a thing they clipped on my finger, and they also had a similar gizmo to check for carbon monoxide in my blood. After the second check, they seemed happy with the results.

The doctor didn't want to give me anything for sleep because he didn't want a sedative decreasing my blood oxygen. Big bummer, because I could have definitely used an Ambien. Shoot, I would have taken a glass of warm milk and some melatonin at this point. I was the kind of tired that surpassed the ability to sleep, and as I looked at the clock, I reckoned I'd been awake now for almost twenty-two hours. I tried to relax, but I missed my furry bedmate. I missed her soft snore and snuggles. The hospital bed felt cold in comparison. It didn't help that someone, whether it was Donnie's killer or someone else, had tried to poison me. It felt like an extreme reaction to my involvement in the investigation. Maybe I'd rubbed the wrong psychopath the right way.

I rubbed my arms to knock down the goosebumps. Could it be that simple? I tried to think of who might hate me enough to want to see me dead. Naomi would have topped my list, but honestly, I didn't think she hated me. I think she saw me as a scoop, a storyline, a notch in her career bedpost, so to speak.

But maybe I was wrong. After all, Tom Jones hadn't been the only killer in his family. His wife Bridgette had been just as guilty, and she took her life after I'd confronted her about Katherine Kapersky. Naomi and Bridgette had been best friends in high school. What if Naomi blamed me for Bridgette's suicide? Even so, was that motive for murder?

I pushed my thoughts from my almost-tragedy and focused my sleep-deprived brain on what I knew about Donnie's death. He was a blackmailer, I don't think there could be any doubt about that. But of how many people? And how long had it been going on? Maybe an earlier victim got tired of paying or couldn't pay anymore. Or maybe it was a new victim who had no intention of ever paying Doyle.

We still didn't have a medical examiner's report. I supposed that wouldn't happen until today. I blinked. It was officially Sunday. Parker and I had a date. I wanted to call my BFF from back home, Hazel. She would have rushed here and brought a healer witch with her in the process, even if the only healer witch was her soon-to-be mother-in-law and longtime nemesis. That's how much she loved me. But I couldn't rely on witch magic or Shifter bonds if I wanted to live in the human world. Which meant I would just have to wait this out.

I opened my eyes when I heard the knock on the door. It opened right after. I expected it to be the nurse, but instead, it was a short, curvy brunette in peach scrubs. Oh. This was Shelly, Jerry's wife.

"Hey." She had a slight diphthong in her accent, which put her origins farther south than the Bootheel. "I hope I'm not disturbing you."

"No." I waved her inside. "You can come in. I'm not sleeping." I recognized the woman right away from the bar and the video. I tensed, ready for flight or fight if this wasn't a friendly visit.

"Your nurse, Laura, told me you were struggling to rest." She smiled. "You're Lily Mason, right? I'm Shelly Atwell."

I thought about her starring role in Donnie's blackmail video, and I hoped that the sheriff's department would be discreet. The women Donnie had filmed were victims, even as they were suspects. I wondered if he'd blackmailed them all or just the ones with something to lose. I thought about Rachel. She'd wanted Donnie's love, and she'd obviously cried her eyes out when he died. Surely, if he had been extorting her for money, she wouldn't have loved him. Maybe Shelly had loved Donnie, too.

"My husband Jerry volunteers at the shelter with you."

Shelly's twang brought me back to the present, and I realized I hadn't responded to her greeting. "It's nice to meet you. Jerry is amazing with the dogs."

She nodded. "He's always been good with animals." She chuckled softly. "It's people he doesn't always get."

I didn't know Shelly and Jerry's home life. For all I knew, he was a terrible husband. Or maybe he was great, and she was terrible. Either way, I wouldn't want anyone taking apart my life brick by awful brick, so I tried to keep my tone neutral and without judgment. "Animals don't criticize or judge. It's easy to love something that you know is going to love you back. People are way more complicated."

Shelly let out a soft laugh and rubbed a birthmark on the back of her hand. "Ain't that the truth of it." She lowered her lashes. "I work in housekeeping here at the hospital. Jerry called me last night after your incident. He asked me to look in on you. I hope you don't mind."

"No, it's sweet." I wanted to ask her about Donnie. Had he come after her for money? To tell the truth, I wasn't exactly sure that he filmed his sexual conquests for blackmailing purposes. Maybe he just wanted to make some personal porn. Either way, yuck. Shelly stood across from me, appearing somewhat fragile. I could use my power on her, but if she had been blackmailed, it might provoke her into doing something rash—like trying to hurt me. People with their backs against the wall were dangerous. "Tell him I'm going to be fine and thank him for taking care of Smooshie until the vet arrived. That made all the difference to me."

Shelly reached her hand back to the door handle. "I best get back to work."

Jerry's wife had been lovely. I'd have to bring him in a box of donuts as a big thank you for last night and for sending his wife to check on me.

*****

The hospital discharged me in the afternoon. Reggie, Nadine, and Buzz had all called to check on me. I told them all I'd be out soon, so they didn't have to come visit. Nadine told me that they didn't have any leads on who blocked my vent, and it looked like the carbon monoxide alarm and the vent had been wiped of prints, though they'd found a partial on the battery I'd found on the floor. However, a partial was hard to match, and it would be even harder if the person didn't have an arrest record.

Parker, who insisted on picking me up, had dropped off a happy, healthy, and carbon-monoxide-free Smooshie with his dad and Elvis before arriving at the hospital. I was on the side of my bed, waiting for the nurse to bring in all my discharge paperwork when he arrived. Dark circles framed his bloodshot eyes.

"You look like you got about as much sleep as I did," I told him.

He quickly strode to me, his hands seizing my upper arms as he drew me into a firm embrace. My arms dangled at my side as he held me so tight, I could do nothing but rest my cheek against his chest.

"I'm happy to see you too," I said with the little breath I had left in my lungs.

He pushed me back from him. "You scared the crap out of me."

"I'm okay," I said gently, feeling suddenly shy under his intensity.

"Let's get you out of here." He grazed the side of my face with his fingertips and tucked an unruly curl behind my ear. "I hate hospitals."

"Just waiting for the hospital to finish up the paperwork." I stared up at him. The way his dark hair fell over his baby-blue eyes made him look more predatory than many of the predators I knew. I inhaled his scent, honey and mint, but not overpowering, just fresh and sweet.

If he were a Shifter, I would swear I was smelling a mate scent. It's something that happens between Shifters who are destined to be together. It had been that way for my mom and dad. And even my best friend Hazel, who was a witch, had developed a mate scent with her husband, Ford, a werebear. But the one thing all Shifters know is that the mate scent isn't possible with humans.

"What are you thinking about?" Parker asked.

I grinned. "How good you smell."

"Seriously? I've been up all night with dogs." He chuckled, and the low, rich sound warmed me to my toes. "Hey," he said. "If you think *Eau de Dog Poop* is attractive, then we really are meant for each other."

"Do I smell like anything, you know, out of the ordinary to you?" I gently bit my lower lip, and half held my breath as I waited for his reply.

He frowned. "No, nothing out of the ordinary. Why?"

The weight of his words—even though I hadn't expected anything more, not really—crushed me. I guess, deep down, I'd hoped that Parker and I would be the exception to the rule when it came to Shifters and humans.

"No reason."

"Unless you count your hair. I haven't told you this, but thanks to your shampoo, I have a thing for cherry-and-vanilla soda, cherry pie with vanilla ice cream, and I even bought a cherry-and-vanilla air freshener for the truck. I'm surprised you didn't notice."

I hadn't noticed. Whenever Parker was around, the only thing I smelled was him. Honey and mint. That's it. "That's so nice," I said, my throat tight. "Do you smell it on me now?"

"Yes. What brand do you use?" When I didn't answer, he asked, "Are you okay, Lily?"

I blinked up at him. "I'm…yes, fine."

My shampoo was juniper and mint, the same brand Parker used. Not cherry and vanilla.

I didn't know how to explain it. I needed to talk to Hazel or Buzz, or both of them, because if I was right, the impossible had happened. Parker had caught my mate scent. And I'd caught his.

Nurse Linda, the day shift ICU nurse, picked that moment to knock and walk in. "I have your paperwork. I just need you to sign a few forms, and we'll get a wheelchair up here and get you on your way."

Parker put his arm around me. "You sure you're all right?"

"Yes," I said, but inside, I was terrified, excited, worried, and elated. Could Parker really be my mate?

*****

On the way to Parker's, Opal Dixon kept circling my thoughts. Buzz had called to tell me that he'd picked up Opal from the sheriff's department last night and taken her home. The hospital, understandably, banned her from entering the premises, and with Pearl still in the hospital, Opal was probably crazy with worry.

"Can we go out to the Dixon place before you take me home?" Those sisters had each other and not much else. If one or the other died, it would be a blow the survivor might not come back from. "I want to check in on Opal. Make sure she's okay."

Parker nodded. "You're a kind woman, Lily. I'm sure Opal will appreciate the visit."

I wasn't as sure as Parker. Opal was headstrong, stubborn, and fiercely independent. She wouldn't want my pity. So, I wouldn't give it to her. I smiled when the crops of flamingos came into view. We parked and walked to the door. It took three knocks before I heard Opal's crusty voice shout, "Just a damn minute!"

She flung the door back, her expression angry and ready to fight. "What do you— Oh, it's you." Her hand, which had been behind her back, dropped to her side. She held the gun from last night. Opal did not play. She waved her non-gun hand at us. "Come on in."

Parker and I followed her inside. "I heard the hospital won't let you back in to see, Pearl. Is there was anything I can do to help?"

"Damn bureaucrats," Opal grumbled. She was just an inch taller than me, so when she turned, we were nose to nose. "Actually, you *can* help. They are keeping Pearl for a few days for observation. Her heart is acting funny. She'll need her makeup, denture cream, hairbrush, and few other things. Oh, and clean underwear. If I give them to you, can you make sure she gets them?"

I nodded. "I sure will."

"Come with me then," she said. "You can help me pack her bag."

"I'll wait here," Parker said.

"Good," Opal replied. "You weren't invited anyhow."

I stifled a chuckle as I followed Opal down the narrow hall. Her trailer was bigger than mine, but it was still a trailer. Pearl's room had a twin bed with a Pepto-Bismol pink headboard. There was also a pink dresser and pink vanity in the small space. The walls had pictures of the Florida coast, palm trees, and real flamingos.

"Pearl really loves Miami," I said.

"She loves the idea of Miami," Opal said. "It's not like she's been there. How can you love something you've never seen before?"

I didn't know how to respond to that, so I asked, "Are you okay? I mean, from last night?"

Opal's dark expression, her furrowed brow as she gathered Pearl's things, concerned me. "I'd be better if I had shot that sorry so-and-so. He had it coming. And at least then I'd understand why the hospital won't let me see my sister." She opened a drawer and pulled out five pairs of folded white underwear and put them on Pearl's bed.

I went to the vanity.

"What makeup will she want?" I opened the drawers of the stand. Lipstick, eyebrow pencils, eyeliners, old mascara, foundations, creams, and more littered the base. I saw an envelope with a mailing address for a Murray Davenport in Las Vegas. It had a stamp on it, reading to send, but the colorful makeup stains around the worn, frayed edges told me it had been in the drawer for a while. And there was something else familiar about the envelope. I looked closer at it.

I recognized the block lettering.

Opal closed the drawer, almost catching my fingers. "That's none of your business."

"Who is Murray Davenport?"

I hadn't meant to, but I must have pushed, because Opal sat down on the edge of the bed, and said, "The son of the man I killed."

I held my breath as the words sunk in. "What happened?"

"I always knew the day would come when I'd be found out. You can't hide from something like this. Not forever." She cackled softly. "Though, for a while, I thought I might get lucky."

"Why'd you kill him?" I had a good idea what the answer might be based on her reaction to Jock the night before. "Was he hitting you?"

Opal shook her head. "Not me." She glanced at a picture on the dresser. It was two young, beautiful women standing by the road in a desert. "Pearl and I grew up in Vegas. She married an older man, Benjamin Davenport, who was an accountant. In the beginning, he was good to her, but it didn't last."

"Is Murray her son?"

"No. He was Benji's from his first marriage. Murray was sixteen and away at boarding school when I shot Benji. That letter is Pearl's apology. Leaving him behind was her biggest regret."

"I'm sorry," I said softly.

Now that Opal had opened up, she kept talking. "I started noticing little things, bruises here and there. Pearl would tell me stories of how she'd tripped or slipped or bumped into this and that. To my shame, I believed her. My sister has always been a klutz. But the day I walked in on him dragging her by the hair across their living room, it triggered something in me I couldn't contain. I knew he kept a gun in the side table in the living room. He was mobbed up, you see. Pearl was crying, begging him to stop. Benji was drunk, and he kept telling her he was going to kill her. I grabbed the gun."

Her hands started trembling almost uncontrollably as she recalled the memory.

"I shot him. I didn't stop shooting until the gun was empty." She met my gaze. "He stopped moving long before that."

"Oh, Opal." My chest squeezed as emotion choked me. "How'd you end up in Moonrise?"

"Pearl wanted Miami, but I knew we had to go someplace where no one would ever look. I picked this town off a map because I liked the name. It turned out Benji had more than one million dollars in his office safe. It was as if fate wanted us to have a fresh start."

"Opal, as far as I'm concerned, your secrets are safe with me. You did what you had to do to save your sister." I only wished I could have done the same for my brother.

"I trust you will, Lily. And if you don't, well, I'm an old woman not long for this place anyhow."

I paused. I had to ask. I had to know. "And the notes?"

Opal gave me a blank look. "The notes?" she repeated.

"The notes that have been going around town threatening to expose people's secrets." Pearl's handwriting was the same as the poison pen's handwriting.

"Oh, *those* notes." Opal looked amused. "It started when Pearl took notice of people like Jock Simmons, getting away with adultery, hurting that poor wife of his and such. I think she wanted to feel like she was doing something important. But then, when she ran out of scoundrels, she just started picking out people she'd met. With her heart condition, her mind's not as sharp as it used to be. Besides, Pearl has always been a little mischievous. I tried to get her to stop, but our pleasures are so few these days."

"But how did she know who has secrets and who doesn't?"

Opal gave me a knowing smile. "Oh, honey. Don't you know? Everybody has secrets."

CHAPTER EIGHTEEN

"I'M NOT AN INVALID," I said as Parker lifted my legs up on the couch and tucked throw blankets around me. I didn't have the heart to tell him that as a Shifter, I usually ran warm. Smooshie wiggled between me and the back of the couch, curling up under my arm. She only added to the heat.

We'd dropped off Pearl's things at the hospital. Parker took them in and made me wait in the car. I didn't tell him about my conversation with Opal. As far as I was concerned, no one would ever find out about their tragic past.

"You just relax," Parker said. "The doctor said you needed to take it easy for a day or two, so that's what you're going to do. And if you give me any trouble, Nadine and Reggie said I could call them for backup."

Uh oh. Calling in the BFF brigade meant serious business. I held up my hands in surrender and Smooshie licked my armpit. "Eww!" I squealed, dropping my arm fast before she could get another good swipe. "Not the pits, Smoosh."

Her tail whacked hard against my legs. I put my arms around her, and she rested her head on my chest.

Parker stared down at us, his face content. "You two are a good match." He grinned. "Never seen a cat and dog get along this well," he teased.

"Har-de-har-har," I said, but I returned his grin. I scratched my girl's ear. She closed her eyes. "She's probably as tired as I am." I yawned as the impact of too much danger and too little sleep settled into my bones.

"Ryan says she's healthy. She got lucky." His expression turned to worry. "You both did."

"It wasn't luck. Smoosh knew something was wrong. She used all her strength to get me moving out of that trailer. I don't know how she managed it, but she saved us both."

"For that..." Parker said, "...she deserves a medal of valor."

"I bet she'd prefer a steak, medium rare."

"You're hungry, aren't you?" Parker asked.

"I'm so tired," I whined. "But yes, I'm starving. The hospital meals were tiny."

"I've never met a woman who could put away food the way you can."

"That's because you've never met a woman like me."

"How about I make you spaghetti for lunch?"

"With cheesy garlic bread?" I asked.

Parker shook his head. "Of course, with cheesy garlic bread."

"That sounds great."

Parker exited the living room and went into the kitchen. Someone knocked on the door. I started to get up, but Parker said loudly, "I'll get it."

I smiled and eased back into the soft pillows he'd placed behind me. I'd always been the caretaker, but since my parents' death, I'd never had anyone take care of me. Not like this. It felt nice. Safe. Weird. But I could definitely get used to it.

I heard Parker open the door and then I caught the low murmur of Theresa Simmons' greeting. Goddess, what she must have gone through last night with Jock's arrest. "Can I talk to Lily?" Theresa asked, her voice soft with worry.

"Just a minute." Parker walked around the corner, but before he could say anything, I nodded.

"I'll talk to her."

An amused smile twitched his lips. He went back to the door. "Come in. Lily's in the living room."

Parker went back to the kitchen as Theresa walked into the room. She rushed over to me and leaned down for a quick hug. "It's so awful," she said. "I heard what happened last night. Are you okay?"

"I'm feeling much better, thanks."

Theresa grabbed the rocking chair from near the fireplace and pulled it over to sit next to me. "I've been worried about you."

"Thanks. I'm fine, really. How did you hear about me?" I asked. "Oh, probably your dad. He was on the scene."

"No." She cast her gaze down to her hands. "Keith told me. Parker asked Keith to come in to volunteer today with Addy because he was taking the day off to take care of you." She gave me one of those secret knowing smiles. "I've never seen that man take any time off for anyone. He's got it bad. I'm glad to see you all aren't trying to fight it anymore."

In my defense, I had never tried to fight it. Well, maybe a little at the beginning. I didn't say any of that though. "He's been a good friend."

"Yeah, right. Friend."

Two could play this game. "What about you and Keith? I thought you two had called it quits."

Theresa looked surprised. "We...had. A couple of months ago, Jock found out about Keith. He threatened me." She swallowed, hard. I knew right then Jock had done more than threaten—he'd hurt her. "Jock is vengeful..." she continued, "...and I knew he'd go after Keith if I didn't fall in line. Besides, I thought my family drama might ruin my dad's reputation. The sheriff is an elected position. My father runs on conservative family values."

My heart ached for Theresa. Jock could cat around as much as he wanted, apparently. But he saw his wife as a possession, not a person. And a controlling, alcoholic abuser wouldn't tolerate anyone else playing with his toys. I didn't like Sheriff Avery, but I couldn't believe he'd want his daughter trapped in a miserable marriage just so he could keep his job.

"Jock hit Lacy Evans last night in front of everyone in the emergency room. My dad arrested him." Theresa smiled softly. "If my dad was willing to arrest my husband and put him in jail in front of God and everyone, I knew he didn't give a crap about what people thought. Right is right."

I didn't want to have a warm fuzzy about Sheriff Avery, but I couldn't deny he loved his daughter—and he was a decent sheriff. Not that I would ever admit that out loud.

"So, you finally told him about Jock's abuse?"

She flinched. Then she took a big breath and looked me in the eyes. "I told Dad everything. He was fit to be tied. He wanted to know why I hadn't told him sooner. It's hard to explain. A guy hits you, you leave, right?"

"It's not that easy," I said.

"No, it's not. Jock stripped away who I was. It's not just him hitting me. It's him telling me that I'm fat and lazy and worthless. It's like...poisoning me every day. I started to believe him. Who would want me? Who would put up with me? I was lucky to have Jock." She dropped her head. "I was so ashamed, so humiliated."

"And then you met Keith?"

Her eyes lit up. "He made me feel so good. He complimented me. He built me up instead of tearing me down. He made me remember the old Theresa. The woman I'd been before I'd married Jock. I never told him, you know—about Jock's abuse. Keith's noble enough to try to do something stupid."

"Are you going to talk to him again?"

Theresa's face went bright red. "He heard about Jock's arrest, and he showed up on my doorstep. I asked him to forgive me—and then I told him everything, too. He said there was nothing to forgive. He wants to help me, Lily. He loves me, and I love him."

She reached out to pet Smooshie and got her fingers cleaned with a pittie tongue bath. "He asked me to move in with him. He lives in a trailer. But you know what? I'd rather live in an outhouse with Keith than in a mansion with Jock."

I took her hand and squeezed it. "What's next?"

"Filing for divorce. Get counseling. Picking out curtains for a very tiny kitchen window." Theresa laughed as she stood up. "I told Parker I wouldn't keep you, so I won't. I just wanted to make sure you were all right."

"And I'm glad you're all right, too." I really felt like making a nighttime feline visit to Jock. I wouldn't kill him. Just maim him a little.

She gave me a quick peck on the cheek and gave Smooshie a final smoosh. "Will you be working this week? If you can't, let me know. I'll take the extra shifts." She shook her head. "I'll need the money."

"I'll let you know."

After she left, Parker stepped in. "Spaghetti will be ready shortly."

"Hurray," I said with real enthusiasm. My stomach growled loudly like one of those velociraptors in *Jurassic Park*, to emphasize just how excited I was for food.

"Did you say hurry?" Parker teased.

"Close enough." I grabbed a small throw pillow from the floor and chucked it across the room as Parker dodged it easily and headed back into the kitchen.

Ten minutes later, he carried in two large plates of spaghetti. Smooshie's ears perked up, and she stood, planting her feet on my stomach as she launched herself to the floor to investigate what kind of food Parker held.

He laughed. "This is not for you," he told her. "Your food is in the kitchen." Elvis stood up. He was tall enough that his head bumped one of Parker's hands, and it turned into a comical game of keep-away from the curious noses before he was able to safely hand me my plate. He sat on the couch with me.

"I made it extra saucy. Just the way you like it."

He'd also put four pieces of cheesy garlic bread around the towering mound of pasta. "Yum." I shoved three large bites into my mouth before I noticed he was watching me eat. "Stop it," I said, not caring that my mouth was full.

Parker shook his head and smiled. "You're an amazing woman."

"Because I can put away a large plate of food in under ten seconds? If I had known that's all it took to impress you..." I let my words trail off and went in for another bite. "This is so delicious."

"My secret recipe," he said. "Well, mine and Ragu's. And I meant what I said, you're amazing, and not just because of your ability to eat your weight in food."

"I'm not that amazing." I scarfed on the cheesy bread as if I hadn't eaten in a week.

"You managed to pull yourself together when your parents died to work, take care of your brother, and finish school. And, when it had to be the scariest prospect in the world, you moved away from everything you know to start a new life for yourself. That's seriously amazing."

I put my plate on the end table and scratched my head. "Uhm, about school." My adrenaline kicked in, and I took a deep breath to steady my nerves.

Parker noticed. He set his plate down on his lap and took my hands. "You're shaking. What's wrong, Lily? There isn't anything you can't tell me."

"I didn't graduate from high school," I blurted out. "I don't know why I didn't tell you. It's dumb. I just, I don't know, I didn't want you to see me as someone not smart enough to finish her senior year. I had to work full time, and I knew I wouldn't be able to go to college, not with Danny to care for. So, I quit. I could have finished, but I didn't. I gave up. Oh, Goddess," I groaned. "I'm a quitter."

Parker sat still in what I could only imagine was stunned silence. After a second, a loud snort blew from his nose, and then he went into full-on belly laugh.

"I'm glad my confession amuses you," I said dryly. His laughter had knocked all the nervousness from me and replaced it with irritation. "It's not funny."

"Lily, for someone so smart—" He cupped my face and kissed me. "The fact that you've managed to do all the stuff you've done without a high school diploma is even *more* amazing."

"I took my GED yesterday. That's what I've been doing all these months. Not prepping for the ACT."

"You did this yesterday?"

"Seven freaking hours." I can't believe it was only yesterday. It felt as if I'd lived through an entire week in one day.

"How'd you do?"

"I'm sure I blew it. It was the reason I pushed our date until today. I knew I'd be tired. I wanted to be at my best for you."

"You at your worst is better than I ever hoped for."

Goddess, that man had a way of making my heart skip a beat. "You're not disappointed?"

"Are you kidding? I'm in awe. When do you find out about the results?"

"Tomorrow. I could wait a week for a letter, but they'll post the results in the afternoon at the GED testing center on campus. I don't want to wait."

"Do you want me to come with you?" He still had ahold of my hands as he waited for my answer.

"I'm not sure I want you there if I didn't pass. I like to ugly cry by myself."

"I want to be there because you *are* going to pass, and when you do, we're going to celebrate."

I tightened my grip on his then nodded. "Okay. You can come."

"Good." He grinned. "It's settled then."

A crash had both of us jumping up. Smooshie was on the other end of the coffee table, wearing a spaghetti wig and holding a piece of cheesy bread between her teeth.

My mouth dropped open as Smooshie practically inhaled the bread, all the while looking at me as if she hadn't just killed my dinner.

Parker began to laugh again. "You better clean her up. I'll get the floor."

I turned to apologize to him, only to find him holding his phone and videotaping Smooshie in all her glory. I scooped the spaghetti off her head, admonishing her to not eat any since it had onions and other things that could irritate her belly. Helpful Parker kept recording the whole thing.

As I took Smooshie back to the bathroom while Parker followed after with his phone held in our direction, something occurred to me about Donnie Doyle.

I hadn't seen a cell phone at his place. Maybe it had video on it like what was on the drives. It would make sense with today's mobile technology. Had the police found the phone? Nadine hadn't said so, but

Sheriff Avery might be keeping stuff back from her because of me.

I turned on Parker as he stood out in the hallway still capturing the moment. I smiled. Waved goodbye. Then closed the door between us.

"This is going on the shelter's social media page," he said through the door. "If this doesn't make people want a pit bull, I don't know what will."

"But won't they be disappointed when they realize this one already owns someone," I said as I turned on the water. Smooshie, who loved baths, jumped right in. I rubbed her ears with both hands. "Don't you, girl. You already own me." At least she owned my heart. I looked at the closed door. Well, she co-owned it, anyhow.

CHAPTER NINETEEN

WE ARRIVED AT THE CAMPUS at ten-thirty in the morning. Classes were in full swing as students prepared for finals week. Parker took my hand as we entered the GED center.

"I'm all right," I said.

"I know." The soft swoop of his eyelashes made my stomach flutter. "I just want to hold your hand, okay?"

"Okay." Walking down the hall toward Ms. Lovell's room, my pulse quickened with my breath. My legs felt like two lead weights that I had to drag along. I caught a look in Parker's eyes that threatened he would scoop me up and carry me if I didn't hold it together.

Ms. Lovell had a message board outside her office door where she'd posted scores revealed by the last four digits of the students' social security numbers. I stopped and sat down on a cushioned bench in the corridor.

"Are you feeling all right? You're not light-headed, are you? The doctor warned that could happen today."

I shook my head. "Nothing like that." I leaned the back of my head against the cool concrete wall. "Can you go look? I don't think I can do it." Not finishing high school had been a huge regret in my life, and this exam had taken on an overwhelming importance.

"Are you sure you want me to do it?"

"Good or bad news, I'll see it on your face. Then we can get out of here."

Parker, his brow furrowed, narrowed his gaze at me. "What's your number?"

"Six four three eight."

He strolled to the board, his expression all business as he scanned the exam scores. Unfortunately, his expression never changed, so when he looked at me, I said again, "Six four three eight."

"I got it the first time," he said.

"Is it not up there? Oh my gosh, I did so bad I didn't even earn a score?"

His eyes sparkled. "You passed. According to the bottom of the paper, your official results will be mailed to you."

"Did you say I passed?"

"Yep." A smile lit up his face. "Congratulations, graduate."

I leapt from the bench and wrapped my arms around Parker. Then I started sobbing.

He froze in place for a moment then stroked my hair in a soothing gesture. "I told you. You're awesome."

I pulled my face back from his shirt before I snotted all over him. "That was weird. I don't know why I'm crying."

"Because you're happy," Parker said. "You conquered a big goal, and now, we celebrate. Where do you want to eat? We can do someplace in town, or we can drive to Cape Girardeau. Whatever you want, Ms. GED Smasher."

"I did smash it," I said. I saw Ms. Lovell go inside her office. "I'm going to go thank my teacher." I sniffled. "She really got me through the course." Plus, I needed tissue. Lots of tissue. "I'll be right back."

I could hear Ms. Lovell talking to someone as I approached the room. Mr. Kirkshaw.

I'd only watched the first few minutes of the video, but I wasn't keen to hear them finish what had been started on there. Mostly, it wasn't my business.

But then I heard Mr. Kirkshaw say, "It's too late, Sally. The police have the drive that Donnie used to blackmail me. It's only a matter of time before they find out about the money we took. We have to go before the police come for us."

Oh, my Goddess! Kirkshaw knew about the memory stick, and he and Ms. Lovell were stealing money.

"Where would we go, John? You gave that kid half our money. Besides, who will take care of Anthony and Cleopatra?"

"For heaven's sake, Sally. I'll buy you new plants."

"You bought those jasmine plants for me two years ago. I just gave them their spring pruning." I could hear the catch of despair in her voice.

"Where it blooms wild," Kirkshaw said softly. "Like our love."

"What are you doing?" I jumped at Parker's voice in my ear. He'd snuck up on me while I was eavesdropping.

I put my fingers to my lips. "Shhh. I'm listening," I whispered.

Ms. Lovell said, "I thought you had a plan to get the money back?"

"I found the receipt in Doyle's drawer for the collar with the memory stick, but I couldn't get that damned box open at the kennel."

I turned to Parker, my eyes wide. "Kirkshaw is the one who tried to break into the shelter," I said with quiet shock. "You better call the police."

"And tell them what? That you overhead something through a metal door that no normal human could hear?"

I grimaced. He had a fair point. I backed Parker away from the door as we were starting to draw stares from students passing by. "Kirkshaw has been in Doyle's house. He saw a receipt for the dog collar Tino wore. I'm not sure how he was stealing money, but he's the head of financial aid. I'm sure he figured out a way."

I pulled out my phone and called Nadine. "You need to come to the college," I told her. "I'm pretty sure I've discovered Donnie's killers."

*****

Parker and I sat on the bench, waiting for Nadine to arrive. Nadine told me that they'd discovered an incriminating conversation between Kirkshaw and Lovell about the embezzlement on the video driver, and that the sheriff had been on the phone with a judge to issue a warrant for the couple's arrest. She'd also told me not to stick around, of course, but I figured I was safe enough with Parker there. Besides, I had a perfectly legitimate reason for being out in the hall. I was one of Ms. Lovell's success stories. All this was how I'd rationalized staying with Parker.

"You know…" he said, "…you snore almost as loud as Smooshie."

"Is this your idea of small talk?"

He shrugged. "Maybe."

"I don't snore."

"Elvis and I beg to differ. Once you snored so loud, you almost woke yourself up."

I raised my brow at him. "I don't know whether it's sweet or creepy that you were watching me sleep."

He tilted his head toward me. "Let's go with sweet."

The door opened to Ms. Lovell's room. Her face was red with worry and registered surprise when she saw Parker and me sitting across the hall. "Lily," she said. "What are you doing here?" Mr. Kirkshaw stood behind her. He looked like a man who could use a good laxative. Super constipated.

"Getting my test results," I said.

"Oh, yes, that's right," Ms. Lovell said. "How did you do? We get numbers, not names."

I grinned. "I passed."

She strode across the hall to me and clasped my hand. "Congratulations. That's wonderful. I knew you could do it."

Aww. My heart clenched. I didn't want Ms. Lovell to be the killer. I really liked her. "All thanks to your great tutoring skills."

"You're going to make an excellent college student. An asset to Two Hills."

Gosh. I'd never felt so conflicted. Was it bad that I wanted to give Ms. Lovell a head start? No. Nope. It didn't matter how nice she was, she and Mr. Kirkshaw had been stealing from the college, or maybe even the students themselves. Being nice didn't make what they did right. And Donnie, no matter what he'd done, didn't deserve to be killed to keep their secrets.

"We need to go, Sally," Mr. Kirkshaw said. He put his hand on her hip and guided her away from me.

"Wait," I said. "Uhm, Mr. Kirkshaw, when should I come in to fill out financial aid forms for the fall semester?" I'd already filled them out on the FAFSA website back in February on Ms. Lovell's advice, but he didn't have to know that.

"As soon as possible. Cut off for the fall is May twenty-fifth." He took a step away from Parker and me. "Now we really have to go."

"When is your office open?" I asked. "I mean, is it open today? Can I go fill out the paperwork now?"

"Yes, yes," he said, annoyed, his veiny nose turning even redder. "Now, I'm sorry to cut this short but—"

"Are you heading there now? Can I just follow you?"

"No, Ms. Mason, you may not follow us!" His eyes widened, and I could see a tinge of yellow. Most likely he suffered from cirrhosis of the liver. I don't know what Ms. Lovell saw in this guy. She could certainly do better.

Note to self: don't play matchmaker with a killer.

"But—"

"No," he said. "No more. Come on, Sally."

Nadine and Bobby barreled down the hallway toward us. I breathed a sigh of relief.

"John Kirkshaw," Bobby said as he put the man in cuffs. "You are under arrest for embezzlement and conspiracy to commit fraud."

Nadine had said the same thing to Ms. Lovell, and the couple was read their rights. Students gathered in the hallway watching the scene as if they were on their own episode of *Live PD*.

"What's going on?" Ms. Lovell asked. "What is going on? John? You can fix this, right?"

"Don't say anything, Sally," he said, struggling as Bobby ushered down the hall. "Just keep quiet. I'll take care of this. I promise!"

After they left, I looked at Parker. "That was interesting."

"Life around you is always interesting." He put his arm around my shoulder. "I think I promised you a celebration."

"I could really go for some more of that spaghetti of yours."

He gave me a new look, one that involved heat and promise. "So, back to my place then?"

A shiver of excitement ran through me. "We never did get to have our date."

"Then we're due."

*****

I sat at the kitchen table, sipping lemonade, while Parker pulled ingredients from the cupboard. The view from my vantage point was pretty spectacular.

"Are you staring at my butt?" Parker asked.

I grinned. "Maybe."

He struck an awkward pose that gave me an even better view. I snorted lemonade through my nose. "Ouch," I said, still laughing as the citrus drink burned my nostrils.

Parker brought me a paper towel. I stood up as he wiped my face. "First time drinking?" he asked. Then he kissed me in a way that stole my breath. One of his hands cupped the back of my neck while the other encircled my waist and pulled me close.

The scent of honey and mint surrounded me. Parker drew back from the kiss and held me to his chest. "Goddess, I love the way you smell."

Parker sniffed my hair. "And you smell like dessert. How is that possible? You used my shampoo this morning."

"I don't know how, but I'm happy I do."

His fingers laced my hair as he drew back to look down at my face. "What do you mean?"

"There is something about Shifters that I didn't tell you." Well, in all honesty, there was a lot about Shifters that I hadn't told him. "When we find the perfect mate, something happens to our body chemistry that causes the mate to have a very distinct scent. It usually only happens between Shifters and Shifters, or Shifters and witches. Shifters can't develop a mate bond with a human." I blinked up at him as he listened. "This must all sound crazy to you."

"I know you're real, Lily. I have no reason to not believe you." He caressed my face. "Only, if you can't have that bond with a human, then how do you explain us? Because I've been smelling this scent since we first ran into each other at that four-way stop."

"Well, there's something else about me that I haven't mentioned."

He raised his eyebrows. "I have a feeling I could spend the rest of my life with you and never know everything about you."

"Would that bother you?"

"If I got to spend the rest of my life with you, I would die a happy man." He kissed me softly. "I don't care about the rest."

"Then you won't be too surprised when I tell you that my great-grandmother was a witch, and that because of that witch, I have a little magic in me."

"Nope, that would surprise me." He chuckled. "What kind of magic?"

I glanced away. "You know how people always seem to tell me their secrets?"

"It does happen a lot."

"That's the power. I'm like a walking, talking lie detector. I get a weird tingle when someone lies, or they aren't telling the whole truth. But unless someone seriously doesn't want to tell me something or they're a sociopath, they generally just tell me the truth."

"So you think being part witch might be making the difference in the whole mate-scent thing?"

"Maybe. I'm not sure. But I'm going to consult with my friend back home. She might be able to get me answers. Because you shouldn't be able to smell the mate scent. Not as a human, but you do, so it has to be possible. I'd been thinking of my witch magic as a curse, but now—"

"Does it work on me? Can you tell if I'm lying?"

It hadn't ever registered with Parker before, so I wasn't sure. "Have you lied to me?"

"No."

I touched his chin. "We can test it. Tell me a lie."

"I don't love you."

My stomach pinched. It didn't register as a lie. "I hope that wasn't the truth."

"I guess we know your stuff doesn't work on me then, because even a blind man can see I'm in love with you, Lily Mason." He kissed me again as I stumbled back, hitting my heel on the dining room chair.

"Ow," I muttered, then planted my lips against his before he could stop to ask me if I was okay. I'd waited a lifetime for a man like Parker. Someone honest, kind, and loving, and it didn't hurt that he was ruggedly handsome.

His hands began to roam my body as I pressed myself against his chest, trying to get as much of me touching as much of him.

His eyes were wild as he lifted me onto the drainboard and placed his hips between my thighs.

"I love you, Lily. I love you so much. I was a fool to not tell you sooner. To not act sooner. Can you forgive me?"

"Yes," I said breathlessly. "I love you too."

He kissed me again, which made my head spin.

Without warning, Parker lost his footing, his forehead hit mine, and the back of my head hit the cabinet handle behind me.

"Christ," he said, holding me as he stabilized himself.

I rubbed the back of my head as Smooshie put her paws up on the counter next to me, her tongue lolling out the side of her mouth. I swear she was laughing.

I knew immediately what had happened. "What did I tell you about putting your nose up people's butts?"

Parker rubbed my forehead with his. "She's got lousy timing."

"Your bedroom door shuts, doesn't it?"

"Yes, it does," Parker said quickly. I squealed with pleasure as Parker scooped me up into his arms and carried me out of the kitchen and down the hall.

CHAPTER TWENTY

PARKER AND I HAD MADE love, several times, over the course of the day and night, pausing only for occasional food and toilet breaks, you know, for Elvis and Smooshie. I woke up the next day happy and exhausted.

And alone.

I must have slept like the dead because I hadn't heard Parker get up. I attuned my ears to the house. I heard cups clink in the kitchen followed by the scent of coffee. I threw on the T-shirt Parker had worn the night before, and I suddenly understood why women in all those romance movies and books walked around in their lovers' clothes.

I closed my eyes and inhaled deeply, hugging the shirt to my body.

"That's got to be the sexiest thing I've ever seen," Parker said.

I opened my eyes and stared. Parker wore blue boxer shorts and nothing else. "You should see the world from my point of view then. I got you beat."

He handed me a cup of coffee then dipped his head for a kiss. "Good morning."

I purred.

Stop it, I told my cougar. *No purring allowed when in human form!*

My kitty did not care, as memories of all the wickedly naughty things I'd done with Parker the night before flipped through my brain like a greatest-hits slide show.

"Nadine called earlier. She wanted you to call her back as soon as you got up."

I blushed. "Does she know…"

"I told her all about last night. Every nitty-gritty detail," Parker said. "Because that's the kind of friendship I have with Nadine."

I rolled my eyes. "You're mean."

"I told her you hadn't slept well, so I wanted to let you rest."

Smooshie bounded into the room, and I handed Parker my cup as she came in for a landing on the bed. She butted my hand with her head, then settled down next to me, her body against my hip as she panted. "I think someone didn't like being kept out of the bedroom last night."

Parker grimaced. "My couch is going to need to be re-stuffed."

"You're kidding."

"About the couch? Nope. Not even a little bit."

"I'm sorry, Parker." I looked at Smooshie with a critical eye, and she licked it. I blinked rapidly. "Smoosh!"

He laughed. "I'd let her eat a dozen couches for ten minutes of last night. It was worth any destruction that occurred."

"Then I don't have to pay for a new couch?" I wiped my brow. "Whew. You see, I work for this guy who doesn't pay me hardly anything."

Now Parker rolled his eyes. "Call Nadine."

I loved on Smooshie for a few minutes, played some tug-o-war with her, and let her chase a ball before I called Nadine. My baby girl had a lot of pent-up energy, and I'd found it was best to wear her out a little before it turned into more couch-eating disasters.

Nadine answered her phone on the first ring. "It's about time," she said. She sounded excited and angry all at the same time.

"Did something happen with the Doyle case?"

"No. We're checking alibis right now, but that's not why I called. We found out whose print was on the battery of your carbon monoxide detector." She paused for dramatic effect. "Seth Grossman."

The name rang absolutely zero bells. "Who?"

"Seth Grossman, but that's not the important part."

"He tried to poison me. I think that's important."

"No. The important thing is that he knows he's a sinking ship, and he's taking all the rats with him." She took a deep breath. "Tom Jones hired him to take care of you, Lily."

"What? How is that even possible? Tom's in jail. It's not like he has access to his bank account, or he can put out an ad for cheap hitmen."

"Seth has a record a mile long for petty crimes. Tom did some dental work for Seth a few years back."

"Surely, I wasn't killed for a free root canal."

"I haven't told you the really good part." She sounded almost giddy.

"Well, tell me already!"

"Seth says Naomi Wells is the person who contacted him and put him in touch with Tom."

Alarm bells rang in my head. "No way!"

"Yes way. The problem is, we can't prove Naomi knew what Tom had planned with Seth. He got paid anonymously with a blank envelope full of cash in his mailbox. He can't say for certain that Naomi dropped off the cash."

"What do you need from me?"

"How do you feel about a sting operation?"

"How much was my life worth?"

"Two thousand dollars. Half up front, the other half upon delivery."

"Wire me up and get ready for a full confession."

"I knew you'd be on board." Nadine laughed. "Oh, I can't tell you how long I've waited for the day Naomi Wells eats crap."

"From the moment I met her, sister. From the moment I met her."

*****

"You might want to wear a loose top, Lily. Or get breast implants," Nadine said.

"Shut up."

Naomi had given me her card with her number on it when she'd blackmailed me for an interview. When I called, she jumped at the chance to meet up. I'd arranged with Nadine to use Buzz's office at noon, leaving me enough time to shower and change clothes. Buzz's office at the diner was private but cluttered enough that we could hide a small camera without it getting noticed. I showed up an hour early, and Nadine wired me up just like I'd seen on *Law &*

Order. Microphone taped between my small boobs and transmitter taped right under.

She snickered. "So, you and Parker, huh? Was kissing involved?"

I didn't answer her.

"Oh ho. More than kissing!"

I blushed. Smooshie, who I'd brought along for moral support, wagged her tail so hard she could give Shakira a run for her money. Those hips didn't lie. My big beauty was happy to spend time with Momma. I think she'd been feeling a little neglected the past couple of days.

"I can hear you," Bobby Morris said over the radio.

"Crap, sorry, Lily," Nadine said. "I guess the transmitter's working."

"Loud and clear," Bobby confirmed.

"If all goes well..." I told her, "...we'll celebrate tonight at Dally's with Reggie, and I will tell you both all about it. Now go be inconspicuous somewhere before Naomi arrives."

Buzz knocked at the door. "She's here."

"She's early," Nadine said. She crammed her tape and stuff into a bag and raced out the back door.

Buzz raised his brow at me. "This is decidedly not staying out of stuff."

"In my defense, she came at me first."

Buzz ruffled my hair like I was seven years old. I didn't mind the uncle-like gesture. It reminded me that I still had family. "Go get her, tiger."

"Cougar."

He chuckled then tapped his chest and gave me a pointed look. Dang it. I forgot about being miked. "You can send her back. I'm ready."

He took Smooshie by the collar. "Come on, girl. I have some steak treats for you."

Smooshie must have understood the gist because she almost knocked Buzz over, skidding on the tiled floor as she rounded the corner toward the kitchen.

"You are spoiling her," I said.

My uncle grinned and stroked his beard. "Every chance I get."

Buzz left and a minute later, Naomi Wells walked in the room. My whole body buzzed with volatile energy. She shut the door behind her. I didn't like having her between me and the exit. I needed a way to escape if she pushed too many of the wrong buttons. I didn't know how I would explain the video and audio, but the headline would read, *Local Woman Goes Furry and Kills Conniving B*tch*. I inhaled a calming breath and leaned against Buzz's desk.

"Let's get this over with," I said. "And after we're done, I don't ever want to see you again."

"I can't make that promise, Lily. You seem to find yourself at the center of a lot of newsworthy stories." She pulled a chair from the corner, and a stack of napkins that had been perched on the back of the seat fell to the floor. Naomi didn't even blink. She just straightened her skirt and sat down.

I clenched my fists, and my claws sank into my palms. I could smell the blood. *Crap. Crap. Crap. Goddess give me control,* I silently prayed.

"I'm going to record our interview if you don't mind. I find it makes it easier to pull direct quotes, and it makes it harder for the people I interview to say I misrepresented them."

"Because you would never take anything said out of context."

Naomi's smile was feral. My body warmed as my cougar begged to surface. *Nope. Nope. Nope. Hold it together.* "Ask your questions. The sooner we're done, the sooner I can be done with you."

"Okay. Let's start with an easy one. Where did you come from?"

"My mother's womb."

Naomi gave me an exasperated glare. "In what town were you born?"

"Burlington, Iowa," I said, regurgitating the town Hazel had put on my forged birth certificate.

"How come there is no record of you before two thousand and six?"

Son of a gun. Naomi had been digging hard on me. What had she found that dated back over ten years though? The forged driver's license maybe. The social security card. Buzz was right, I should have minded my own business when I got to town.

I cracked my knuckles. "I've never been a big fan of having an electronic footprint. My parents died when I was in high school, and I kept to myself." Mixing in some truth made the lie convincing.

Naomi raised a suspicious brow, but she went on to the next question. "Why did you move to Moonrise?"

"Are you trying to set up a dating profile for me or interview me about Tom Jones' arrest?"

"Background is important to a story."

"I think you're full of it."

Naomi leaned forward. "And I think you're a liar, Lily Mason. A liar and a nosy busybody who gets people hurt."

I'd had enough of Naomi and her attitude toward me. I prayed to the Goddess and summoned up every bit of my desire for her to tell the truth and put it into my next question. "Why are you really here, Naomi? What do you want from me?"

"I want you to suffer. To pay for what you did to Bridgette. She was a good person." She shook her head. "No, a great person, and you got her killed."

"I'd say that's some revisionist history," I said. I stood up and moved behind Buzz's desk, so I wouldn't be tempted to claw her eyes out. "You want me to pay, huh?" I pointed an accusing finger. "Is that why you helped Tom hire Seth Grossman to kill me?"

"Yes," she blurted then covered her mouth. "Oh, God." Her expression went from scared to denial to rage. "I hate you!" she screamed and lunged at me. "I should have killed you myself instead of trusting that stupid oaf!"

She was quick, but I was quicker. "Anytime!" I shouted at my chest.

When Naomi came around the desk, I leapt over like the paranormal creature I was, and Naomi staggered back. Then she let out another bellow and took chase as I flung the door open and fled the room. Smooshie passed me in the hall, stopped short of Naomi, and began to *Woof! Woof! Woof!* in a very loud and convincing manner.

"Get that monster away from me!" Naomi cried out, then slammed the door between her and Smoosh, effectively trapping herself in Buzz's office.

Nadine and Bobby pounded on the back door, and I raced back and let them in.

"What took you guys so long?"

"Maybe next time don't lock us out," Nadine complained. "Are you okay?"

"Fine," I said, not even out of breath. Smooshie stood watch at Buzz's door. "Naomi is in the room. Did you get what you needed?"

"Oh, yeah." Nadine grinned. "She is *so* under arrest."

"We're definitely celebrating tonight." I hadn't told her about my GED results yet, and I definitely wanted to dish on Parker, and now that Naomi was out of my hair, I felt like it would be smooth sailing from here on in.

In hindsight, it was a lot of wishful thinking on my part.

CHAPTER TWENTY-ONE

TWO HILLS BREWERY OPENED up on Oak Street where Nix's Bar used to be before it burned down. It had opened recently, but we had avoided going because of the bad memories the place held, like almost losing Nadine and finding a dead body in the alley. However, Reggie, Nadine, and I all agreed that none of us wanted to step foot in Dally's for a while.

The brewery had an eclectic atmosphere, mismatched tables and chairs, a Wurlitzer jukebox with '50s and '60s songs, bare Edison light bulbs dangling from the ceiling and over every table. It was as if the owners went down to the local thrift shop and bought everything but the clothes. Although, the new owner was dressed in vintage jeans with a flannel shirt, and construction boots with splashes of dried concrete on them, so maybe he bought the clothes there too. On top of that, the bartender had a handlebar mustache, fully waxed and curled.

Like I said, eclectic.

Needless to say, the place was wall to wall with people, even more than what usually hung out at Dally's on ladies' night. Reggie had arrived before me and had grabbed a small wooden table that looked like it had been sanded, stripped, but never finished. None of the chairs might have matched, but at least they were of appropriate height for the table. I noticed it was near the kitchen and bathrooms. Ugh.

But as far as I could see there were no other free seats, so she had done the best she could.

She waved at me, and I waved back, making my way past several other full tables to join her. I sat down. "This might be the last time we come here."

Reggie shrugged. "They have karaoke on Friday nights."

"Then we're definitely never coming here again."

We both laughed.

"I heard you had an exciting day," she said. "Nadine filled me in earlier."

"I think I bring out the worst in people."

"That woman was already the worst." She put her hand over mine. "I'm sorry she used me to blackmail you."

"She never really wanted a story from me. She wanted my humiliation. She wanted me to suffer."

Reggie shook her head. "I don't understand how people can be so cruel. Speaking of cruel, my ex told me he's coming in two days before graduation. One extra day to make sure I'm extra miserable."

I nudged her. "When he arrives, we could find his car in the parking lot and key the crap out of it."

"Lily!" She leaned in close. "You're not serious are you, because..."

"Hey, I'm up for any punishment you want to dish out to that jerk." I waved at the barmaid, a perky strawberry blonde, wearing flannel and skinny jeans, and who looked like she might have turned twenty-one that morning.

Nadine joined us at the table. "Who are we punishing?"

"Reggie's ex-monster."

"Well, we should probably keep the punishments legal, unless we take our time to plan it out." She winked. "I'm a cop, Reggie's a medical examiner, and Lily is detail oriented. We could probably plan something so good that no one would even think to look in our direction."

Reggie giggled. "You're terrible. Both of you. Besides, it's my ex-husband, everyone would be looking in my direction."

"You're right," I said. "It's always the spouse or the ex. By the way, did your doctor friend get the autopsy done?"

"Yes, and the results are really strange. He had high chloride levels in his blood and organs, and he had extreme pulmonary edema."

Nadine looked blank.

"His lungs were full of fluid," I told her.

"And he had cardiomegaly," Reggie said.

Nadine glanced at me.

"Enlarged heart."

Nadine smiled. "You're going to be a good nurse or doctor, Lily. Unlike some people who have to use mumbo-jumbo terminology." She cast an accusing glance at Reggie. "Get down to it already."

"Oh, fine," Reggie said. "He died of exposure to chlorine gas."

"Wow," Nadine said. "How does someone get exposed to chlorine gas? Is that like bleach?"

"Mixing bleach and ammonia would do it," I said. "It's why they always warn people not to mix the two solutions together."

Reggie nodded. "Lily's right. But the concentrations of chloride levels in all the internal organs means this was probably industrial-grade chemicals."

The strawberry blonde finally came over to our table. "What can I get you ladies to drink?"

"I'll take a beer," I said.

"What kind?"

"What kind do you have?"

She produced a list that was taller than me of variations of microbrews. I finally settled on one that was called Citrus Fantasy.

Nadine smirked. "That sounds gross."

I wasn't going to argue, because I kind of agreed.

"I'll take a Sizzle Twist," Reggie said. It was a gin and tonic drink with a twist of lemon.

"I'll try your Merry-Go-Cherry."

"Now that sounds gross," I said. It was cherry vodka, lime juice, sugar syrup, and club soda. "You might as well drink a bottle of cough medicine."

Nadine appeared unperturbed. "I like that too." When the waitress walked away, Nadine said, "I think this is a hipster bar."

"Well, la-ti-da," said Reggie. "I guess we're in with the cool crowd."

"If you think hipsters are cool," Nadine snorted.

I was still thinking about the chlorine gas. "Was that why he had those dark marks on his skin?"

"Yes. His skin had actually eroded in the exposure."

I turned to Nadine. "That means—"

"I know what eroded means."

I laughed. "Okay." Hipster barmaid brought us our drinks. I waited until she left to ask Nadine, "Did they find any chemicals at Donnie's house? Or at Kirkshaw's or Lovell's?"

Nadine stretched back and almost tipped her chair over. "Can I say how much I hate this place?"

"Yes," Reggie and I said at the same time.

Safely back on all fours, Nadine continued, "There were no industrial-strength chemicals at either Donnie's or the suspects' houses. Although, Kirkshaw and Lovell might not be suspects for long."

"They're innocent?"

"Not by a long shot. The video revealed the scheme to defraud the school and the government. They have been taking applications from borderline-need students and applying for Pell Grants and scholarships in their name and pocketing the money for themselves."

"That's awful."

"It gets worse. Our forensic accountant reckons they've scammed over a million dollars in the past five years. Donnie was blackmailing Kirkshaw for a piece of the pie."

"What about the women on the videos? Did they know they were filmed? And was he blackmailing them?"

"Not a single one of them." She raised her brow as she stared across the room. "Hey, is that Rita, Richard O'Reilly's wife?"

"The guy that attacked Lily the other night?" Nadine asked.

"Yes."

"I think it is," I said. We watched her skirt the edges of the room to a dark table in the corner. She sat down, but without giving away my Shifter eyes, I couldn't see who she sat with. "Is he still in jail?"

"Yep. Rita denied sending him after you."

Richard had not been lying. He believed with all his might that his wife had been violated and that it had been filmed.

"So, Kirkshaw and Lovell have an alibi for the murder?"

"Looks like they were in Chicago at a work function. The hotel and the organizers of the event confirmed their story." Nadine took a sip of her Merry-Go-Cherry. She cringed. "Yep. Just like cough medicine with a splash of club soda."

I dared to taste the Citrus Fantasy. The dark beer was thick, bitter, with an aftertaste of overripened orange. It wasn't great, but it wasn't as horrible as I'd thought. "I can live with it."

Reggie tasted her drink. "Just the way I like my gin and tonics."

"Did you ever find Donnie's phone?" I asked Reggie. "I didn't see it when I was at his house."

"I know he had one," Reggie said. "He put my number in his phone that night."

"We never found one," Nadine said. "The sheriff insisted on a thorough search yesterday, and other than a jimmied drawer that had several new, in-the-package USB drive and a receipt. There wasn't anything else."

"Not a lone cap?"

"Lily?"

I shrugged sheepishly. "I might have taken a quick look around."

"It's how she found my earring," Reggie said.

"Hey," Nadine was looking toward the far side of the room. "Is that Shelly Atwell getting up from Rita's table?"

Reggie shrugged. "I wouldn't know Rita or Shelly from Eve."

"Wow," I sputtered. "Rachel Keeton, the sheriff's niece, just got up as well." Talk about alarm bells. "Are they all friends?"

"Not that I know of, but if they are, how disgusting was Donnie Doyle?" asked Nadine.

"Hey!" Reggie said.

"Sorry," said Nadine.

"Did he really have sex with all of them?" Reggie looked ashamed and horrified.

"Yes," Nadine and I said.

"That *is* disgusting."

An idea curled inside my mind. "Reggie, can a mild exposure to chlorine gas cause pneumonia?"

"Sure," she said. "It's called toxic pneumonitis. Meaning it's pneumonia that isn't caused by an infection."

"Would the doctors know it wasn't infectious pneumonia if the person diagnosed didn't tell them that she'd been exposed to a chemical gas?"

"No." She frowned. "They would have treated her the way they would treat any pneumonia, breathing treatments, corticosteroids, possibly furosemide."

Nadine held up her hand to me. "Don't even try to explain what Reggie is saying. Just get to the point."

"Shelly Atwell was in the hospital not quite two weeks ago with a bout of pneumonia." I stared at them both expectantly. When they didn't jump on my train of thought, I added, "And she has some discoloration on her hand."

"Oooh," Nadine crooned. "Like Donnie did on his face and arms."

"Exactly. I thought it was a birthmark, but maybe is wasn't."

"Do you think she killed him?" Reggie asked. "On her own?"

"No." I shook my head. "I don't think she did it on her own. I have a feeling she had some help." I turned to Nadine. "Do you think you can track down Donnie's phone number?"

"Why?"

"Because I have a hunch that one of those women have the missing phone."

Reggie pulled out her own phone. "Uhm, I have Donnie's number. What do you want to do with it?"

I pulled a ten out of my purse and dropped it on the table. "I want to call that phone and see if Shelly, Rita, or Rachel ring."

Reggie and Nadine put money on the table as well.

"This is a bad idea," Reggie said.

Nadine grinned. "All the best ones are."

*****

It was a little after eight o'clock when we hit the street.

"Shouldn't we call for backup?" Reggie asked.

"And tell them what?" Nadine waved her hand at Reggie. "All we have is a lot of guessing and conjecture. We don't know that any of those women had anything to do with Donnie's murder. We're just playing a game of 'Test Lily's Theory.'"

"Which usually proves right on the money." Reggie kept pace as we strolled after the trio, but her shoes made a loud clacking noise with every step.

"Jayzus, Reggie, do you have to be so loud?"

"Trailing after suspects wasn't on my to-do list when I put on my high heels tonight."

I smiled at my two friends bickering back and forth. "I had sex with Parker last night."

Nadine grabbed my arm and brought me to a halt. Reggie stopped, and muttered, "Thank God." Then she looked at me. "That we stopped, not that you and Parker had sex. Congratulations."

"Oh my gosh, Lily, talk about burying the lead. That's the first thing you should have told us tonight. I was just teasing you on the phone, but day-yam. You really did it."

"Well, we did it…" I amended, "…like five times."

"I'm not jealous," Nadine said. "Buzz is a beast in bed."

I shook my head. "Ew. T.M.I."

"You just told me about *your* sex life."

"Yeah, but I'm not sleeping with your un…cousin."

"True that." Nadine smiled brightly as we started walking again. The ladies were just up ahead in a public parking lot. "Does this mean you all are an official thing?"

"I think so." I nudged Reggie. "Get your phone ready."

Reggie held it up, and the bright screen illuminated our faces. I slapped a palm over it. "Sorry," Reggie said. She dimmed the screen. "Ready."

"One more thing," I said. "Don't get too loud, but I passed my GED."

Nadine harsh-whispered, "Cheese and rice, Lily!"

Reggie hugged me and bounced on her toes in a happy dance. "You are winning at life, lady."

"Thanks. I'm pretty proud of myself."

"As you should be," Nadine said.

We hugged the buildings on the last block before the parking lot. This close to Shelly, Rachel, and Rita, I could overhear some of the conversation.

"We're fine," Rachel said. "Just stick to the plan. This should be the last time we meet."

"But the police know about us," Shelly said.

"They know we had sex with Donnie, but as long as that's all they think, they'll keep it quiet."

"Jerry can't find out. I... I don't want to hurt him." Shelly toed the ground.

"You should have thought about that when you were boffing a man ten years younger than you." This was Rachel. She sounded angry.

"My husband is in jail because of your bright idea, Rachel! So, you need to shut up and stop acting like you have all the answers."

"Call Donnie's number now," I whispered.

Reggie hit the phone with her finger. "Oh my God, oh my God! It's ringing."

I heard a ringtone sound I didn't recognize and held my breath. Was this it?

Rachel pulled the phone from her purse.

"Why do you have that?" Rita asked. "I told you to toss that in the lake!"

"Who is it?" Shelly asked.

"Hot Doc," Rachel said. "Another one of Donnie's whores."

Reggie frowned. She looked at me, and I shook my head. She hung up, and we backed behind a protruding wall. "I think that confirms Lily's theory," Reggie said. "*Now* can we call for backup?"

Reggie's phone rang. Loudly. The screen lit up with the name "Donnie" across it.

"Oh, no." Reggie tried to turn it off, but her panic made her fumble the phone and it hit the sidewalk. "No!"

"Over there," I heard Rachel say.

"I think they know we're here," Nadine had her own phone to her ear. "This is Deputy Booth 10-10 at

Twelfth Street and Oak, requesting backup to my location for three P.O.Is in a murder investigation."

"They can't find that phone," I heard Rita say. "You have to get rid of it."

"I gotta get Donnie's cell," I said to my friends, then took off running toward the three women with my focus on Rachel.

I knew Nadine and Reggie couldn't have heard the distant conversation, so they wouldn't understand me bolting toward what they considered danger, but I couldn't let Rachel trash the evidence that would put away Donnie's killers.

I heard the clack of Reggie's heels, and the heavier footfalls of Nadine's tennis shoes right behind me. The three ladies saw us coming and split into separate directions at a jog.

"I've got Rachel," I shouted. Shelly seemed the slowest, so I said, "Reggie, you take the one heading toward the bank. Nadine, you get Rita." I didn't give them a chance to argue as I chased down Rachel at top human speed. But when I saw her crouching next to a drain on the road, I kicked it up a notch, engaging my cougar abilities.

The last ten feet, I dove at Rachel, soaring through the air before I tackled her sideways. The phone flew from her hand and skidded across the asphalt. I flipped Rachel onto her back.

"Why," I growled. "Why kill Donnie?"

"Because," she blustered. "I loved him!"

"You don't kill people you love."

"You do when they don't love you back." A sob wrenched from her. "I was searching his phone to see who else he was seeing. I saw the videos. He has them uploaded to his cloud. I couldn't believe it!"

"Why involve Shelly and Rita?"

Rachel stopped crying. "Because I could. I told them that Donnie had video of their sexcapades. I'd downloaded enough to my phone that they believed me. After that, it was easy to convince them. Rita's experience with evidence, Shelly's with chemicals, and my determination, it wasn't hard to plan his death. But when you came to Walmart Saturday, I knew you knew about the videos."

"Actually, I didn't. Is that why Richard O'Reilly came after me?"

"Rita was more than willing to send him to do the dirty work."

If it were possible for smoke to come out of my ears, I'd have been setting off alarms. "So, you guys kill Donnie. Why pose him as if he slipped in oil? Did you plant the blood?"

"He had a seizure and hit his head when he fell. Rita said that the sheriff would call it an accident." She glared at me. "And he *would* have if you hadn't stuck your nose in."

"Or if you all hadn't been dumb enough to put the freaking oil bottle away."

Rachel blanched. She'd been so talkative that I had let my guard down, which was the first lesson in Dumb Moves 101.

Rachel bucked beneath me and got her leg up high enough to kick me in the stomach. The air whooshed from me as I staggered to my feet. Rachel was already running toward the phone. I let more of my cougar out, fur sprouting along my arms, and I did what was humanly impossible. I beat her to it.

I snatched the phone just inches from her grasp. She looked at me and staggered backward. "What? What *are* you?"

"Your worst nightmare." I touched my tongue to a fang. "Try that again, and I will make sure you regret it."

"You're a monster!"

I willed my cougar to recede, and when I knew I was fully back to my human form, I gave Rachel a look of pity. "Oh, Rachel. You're the only monster here."

*****

Rachel gave me no more trouble as we walked back to the parking lot. Deputy Larimore and Deputy Morris were on the scene. They'd taken Rita and Shelly into handcuffs already, and Larimore came and got Rachel. I handed the cell phone over to Bobby and told him it was Donnie's phone. Then I went to stand by my girls who were leaning against a sporty Mustang in the lot.

"Any trouble?" I asked.

"Rita gave me a bit of a chase, but I got her. I had to threaten physical violence to get her to come along quietly," Nadine said. "I'm not sure running on a Merry-Go-Cherry was such a great idea." She pressed her palm into her stomach.

Reggie shrugged. "Shelly gave up before I caught her. I think she was ready for it to be over."

"How did she manage to get a chemical burn and pneumonia when the other two didn't?" I asked, not really expecting an answer.

"She confessed everything," Reggie said. "She stole chlorine, ammonia, and three hazmat suits with hazmat masks from the hospital. Rachel and Rita met her at Donnie's house. While he was at work, they filled the sink with the mixture then waited outside for him to come home. What Shelly hadn't counted on was the puppy. When Donnie took the dog inside, she waited a few minutes then ran inside without her mask on and her right glove off. Donnie was dying as she rescued the dog from the house. The dog ran off. After, they put all their gear on, drained the sink, cleaned the house top to bottom. Shelly said she's very good at her job. And after, they set up the scene to look like an accident."

There was still something I didn't get. "With all the careful planning, why'd they put the oil away? A dead guy can't do that."

"The accident staging wasn't part of the plan. Shelly said she put it away out of habit." Reggie leaned back with a satisfied smile. "I now understand why some people find investigating so thrilling. Though next time I'm wearing sensible shoes."

"Yeah, right," Nadine snorted.

Bobby walked over. "You all need to come down to the station and make a statement."

"We really know how to party," said Reggie.

"I think the next girls' night out needs to be a girls' night in. We wear pajamas, drink wine, and marathon Netflix shows," I said.

"I'm in," said Nadine.

We turned to go, and I breathed a sigh of relief.

No more dead bodies, I told myself.

I wondered if it was a promise I could keep.

CHAPTER TWENTY-TWO

OVER THE NEXT WEEK, a lot of things changed for me. For one, Naomi and Seth agreed to testify against Tom Jones for conspiracy to commit murder. The prosecuting attorney then offered Tom a deal—plead guilty on all charges, and he would get life without parole, or he could try his luck with a jury, but the state would recommend the death penalty.

Tom took life. Yay! I was finally free of Tom Jones.

Adding to that, Rita and Shelly turned hard on Rachel and took deals for twenty-five years in jail. Also, Hazel had relayed my Shifter-witch theory with the powers that be, and she confirmed that it was likely that my magic may have made the mate bond possible between Parker and me. Even better, thanks to our magic-bond, it also meant Parker would enjoy the same long life I had ahead of me.

When I wasn't with Parker or at the shelter, I spent all my free time holding Reggie's hand as she struggled through the last few days before CeCe's graduation. Every time I brought up telling Greer about Donnie, she would make some excuse about party planning, errands, patients, and whatever else she could think of to avoid dealing with her personal life.

Needless to say, the week sped by like a bullet train. Collision course: Graduation.

Parker drove me to the graduation. We arrived early for Reggie, CeCe, and Addy. He was part of our shelter family, and we wanted to celebrate with him, too.

Ryan pulled into the parking lot next to us with Paul Simmons.

"What's Ryan doing with Paul? I didn't know they knew each other," Parker said.

I leaned over to get a better glimpse at Ryan's sports car. Paul brought Ryan's fingers to his lips and kissed them. I smiled. "Yep. They know each other."

"Oh." Parker tucked his chin. "Oh," he repeated. "Okay. I get it now." He looked at me and grinned. He got out of the truck. He gave Ryan's hood a quick slap. "Hey, Petry, you guys coming in?"

Ryan got out of the car, his cheeks flushed. "We're, uh, sure."

I waved at Paul. "Good to see you again."

"You too, Lily." His smile was shy. "How's the house coming along?"

"It's slow but steady," I said. "So nice of you to ask." As we walked into the auditorium, I looped my arm in Parker's. I got up on my tiptoes as we neared the doors and said in his ear. "See, I told you Ryan wasn't interested in me."

Inside, I found Reggie chasing CeCe around with a camera, taking a million pictures of her with her friends in various states of pre-graduation. Where CeCe was, Addy was close by. I gave them both hugs and gave them cards with some cash I'd saved just for this day. "Congratulations, both of you."

"Thanks, Lily," Addy said. "I don't think I would have gotten through this year without you."

CeCe whacked him on the shoulder. "Hey, I'm the one who got you through math."

Addy grabbed her hand when she tried to smack him again. I felt the electricity between them when he didn't let go. Then they were holding hands, and Addy couldn't get the stupid grin off his face.

I went to Reggie. "Alert, alert! Teenagers in lust." I pointed to the intertwined fingers.

Reggie's eyes misted up. "It's about time."

I put my arm around her. "How you holding up? Do we need to bury an ex yet?"

Nadine jumped into the conversation. "The loser keeps trying to talk to Reggie. It's like playing chess, and we keep sacrificing seniors to save the queen."

"It's not that bad. Every time he approaches, I walk the other way."

"And I put three graduates in his path." Nadine smirked. "It only looks easy because the guy behind the curtain is doing all the work."

"Good strategy," I said.

"I'm glad you approve because you're on Roger duty now."

I watched as the seniors around us laughed, snapped selfies, fixed makeup and hair, put messages on their hats, and in general, shared the camaraderie of having this huge common experience. I sighed. I couldn't help it.

"Regina," a tall, lanky man with sandy-brown hair said. He had a long face, a thin nose, and deep-set green eyes that made him...not handsome, but attractive.

Nadine turned on me. "You had one job, Lily. One."

Roger the Douche cleared his throat. "I've been trying to find you all day."

Reggie stiffened. "I'm too busy right now, Roger. I've got important stuff to do for our daughter's big day."

"It's just high school," he said in disgust. Did I say attractive? I meant ugly. Like troll ugly. "You can take two seconds."

"Hello, sweetheart." Greer Knowles, like a knight in a shiny charcoal-gray suit, joined us. He put his arm around Reggie and gave her a look I recognized from when his son was throwing it my way. One-hundred-percent heat. "Sorry I'm late."

I could see the tension leave her face. "It's all right." She leaned in for a kiss. Not a long one, but more than friendly. "I'm glad you're here now."

"I'm Roger Crawford," the man said to Greer.

Greer gave Roger a look that would shrivel a hippo. "So?"

"So?" I could see the wheels spinning in Roger's head. What can you say after something like that? Nothing. Which is what Roger did. He turned on the heel of his expensive Italian loafer and left our little group.

Nadine hooted and high-fived Greer. "Dude. That was seriously badass."

Reggie laughed. "It really was."

Greer gave her another kiss, and he went off to find Parker. "So," I said. "You told Greer about Donnie?"

Reggie nodded. "Yes, I did."

"And I guess it all worked out?"

"Yes." She wiggled her eyebrows in a very un-Reggie way. "It really did."

Nadine and I, along with Parker, Greer, and Buzz, jumped to our feet with Reggie when her grown baby was finally announced.

"Cecelia Lynn Crawford," the announcer said.

We all hooted, hollered, and whistled. We made enough noise to fill a stadium. CeCe's smile was ear to ear as she took her diploma.

"I really wish I would have done this," I said to Parker.

"What's that?"

"You know. Graduation. Walking across the stage. The cap and gown. Everything."

Parker laced his fingers with mine. He dipped his head to whisper in my ear. "I bet I still have my old cap and gown lying around if you want to roleplay a little graduation tonight."

"Can we play 'Pomp and Circumstance'?"

"Anything you want, Lily." Parker chuckled. "And I mean anything."

The End

Paranormal Mysteries and Romances
By Renee George

Peculiar Mysteries
www.peculiarmysteries.com
You've Got Tail (Book 1)
My Furry Valentine (Book 2)
Thank You For Not Shifting (Book 3)
My Hairy Halloween (Book 4)
In the Midnight Howl (Book 5)
My Peculiar Road Trip (Magic & Mayhem)
Furred Lines (Book 6)

Barkside of the Moon Mysteries
www.barksideofthemoonmysteries.com
Pit Perfect Murder (Book 1)
Murder & The Money Pit (Book 2)
The Pit List Murder (Book 3)

Witchin' Impossible Mysteries
www.romance-the-night.com
Witchin' Impossible (Book 1)
Witchin' Impossible: Rogue Coven (Book 2)
Witchin' Impossible: Familiar Protocol (Book 3)
Witchin' Impossible: Mr. & Mrs. Shift (Book 4)

About the Author

I am a USA Today Bestselling author who writes paranormal mysteries and romances because I love all things whodunit, Otherworldly, and weird. Also, I wish my pittie, the adorable Kona Princess Warrior, and my beagle, Josie the Incontinent Princess, could talk. Or at least be more like Scooby-Doo and help me unmask villains at the haunted house up the street.

When I'm not writing about mystery-solving werecougars or the adventures of a hapless psychic living among shapeshifters, I am preyed upon by stray kittens who end up living in my house because I can't say no to those sweet, furry faces. (Someone stop telling them where I live!)

I live in Mid-Missouri with my family and I spend my non-writing time doing really cool stuff...like watching TV and cleaning up dog poop.

Made in the USA
Columbia, SC
25 May 2020